ONE SEASON BOOK TWO

# THE UNDERGROUND

A Novel

by

EJ FLYNN

1

One Season Book Two: The Underground by EJ
Flynn
ILF Publishing/September 2019

Published by ILF Publishing
Mamaroneck, New York

*Book design by EJ Flynn*

A signed limited edition has been privately printed by
ILF Publishing

Printed in the United States of America
Published simultaneously in Canada and Europe

www.ILFPublishing.com
ISBN: 978-1-688-549418 - Paperback

3

For my mom and dad without whom I would not be here today. Thank you for always believing in me and providing me with the courage to follow my dreams. I love you with all my heart.

## **Prologue**

"It's true, it's actually happening. The End is near. My children, we have to find our way to our new world. Follow me, my flock, I will lead you to salvation. Vow your loyalty to me and I will prepare you for the Rapture."

A large crowd formed around a man with long, scraggly, blonde hair, dressed in a long white robe and sandals. His arms spread wide standing at a makeshift pulpit in the middle of Greenwich Village.

"Where? Where are you taking us?" A man yelled over the noise of the busy Manhattan street.

Others walking by the scene paused a moment,

quickly losing interest as New Yorkers often did, and moved on.

"Dare you question your Savior? Have I ever led you astray before? Have I ever given you reason to doubt me? So be it then, stay, stay here and deal with what is to come. The Rapture will only save those who are righteous. Only those who are faithful. With faith, you do not question. With faith, you believe what you cannot see. You follow without doubt."

"Forgive me, Abraham, I will follow you wherever you lead." The man knelt on one knee in a deep bow.

"You do not have to do what I say, we are all blessed with free will, even the non-believers." He dismissed the man with a wave of his hand.

"You are all free to stay. All those without faith, you may stay here. I do not wish to save non-believers. The Rapture would not save you, so why should I.

Stay here and meet your fate. The rest of you, we must prepare, prepare to go underground to our new world, Sub Terra."

# Chapter 1

## *HUTCH ALEXANDER*

It was warm. Hot even. We were in what looked like some kind of supply closet. There were hundreds of unlabeled silver canisters. There was warmth coming from a vent in the wall. A flickering light above us hissed, and we heard sounds outside the one door in the room.

"Did you hear that?" It sounded like a child.

"Yeah, do you think we caught one?" Anne and I looked at each other. What could they be talking about? Why were there children there? I had so many questions running through my head.

"Caleb! Get away from there." It was a woman's

voice. "You know you're not allowed back there."

"Sorry, mom. C'mon, let's go, we'll sneak out later and see what we caught." There were shuffling steps, and then silence.

"What is this place?" Anne asked me.

I, of course, had no idea. We waited in silence a while longer, then decided to try opening the door, the Staties in pursuit of us forgotten. The door had a knob on it, not like the doors in the Tyson Estate. The metal knob was warm to the touch. It turned easily and opened into a hallway. I took Anne's hand, and we ventured out into the dimly lit hallway. Silently, we explored. It looked nothing like the hallways in the Estate. The walls were white, the floors carpeted and spongy under our feet, in complete contrast from the ground above. I smelled food. We didn't dare talk and give ourselves away to whoever was there. We moved along to the end of the hallway. Still holding hands, we walked out into a large room. It was empty. We heard voices, and then laughter. Anne looked at me confused.

"Hello?" I shouted into the darkness.

"What are you, crazy?" Anne whispered.

"They don't sound dangerous. It sounds like a family."

They heard me and were instantly silent. We heard someone coming, and Anne seemed to brace herself to be attacked.

"Who's there?" It was a man's voice.

"We're lost, and we don't mean any harm." My voice echoed through the empty room. The man entered the room with a look of confusion, not malice. "I'm Hutch, this is Anne. We sort of fell into your closet from above ground and found our way out here."

"You two must be freezing. Come, come in."

Anne looked at him, wide-eyed. He was not angry we were there. He was welcoming us into his home. We followed him. He led us into what looked like a kitchen. The food we smelled was laid out on a large table, with a woman and two young boys sitting at it. They all looked up and smiled at us.

I smiled back. I looked at Anne, she wasn't smiling. I took her hand and squeezed reassuringly.

The dinner table they sat at was filled with foods I didn't recognize. It all smelled glorious. The man motioned for us to sit down. We sat. I could tell Anne was not comfortable.

"I am Jacob, this is my wife Mary Elizabeth, and those two are our sons Caleb and Holden. We are the Hensley Family.

"Mary Elizabeth, please, set two more places."

She put together plates of food for us and encouraged us to eat.

"What is this place?" Anne asked, before picking up her fork.

I was curious, and anxious to learn more. How did we never know about this place? A whole other race of people we could have been studying. Maybe Eden wasn't the only answer.

Jacob sat down at the head of the table and spoke.

"This is Sub Terra. We are Dwellers, and this is our home, we call our Dwelling. We are one of thirty or so families who live peacefully as God's children, grateful to have what we have and live the way we do. When word of The Shift spread around the world, our savior Abraham Mulcahey brought a congregation of believers underground to escape. The year was 2025. He organized life down here as it was above ground before The Shift. Our way of life, our traditions, are nearly identical to that time. We live a very simple existence down here. And we are safe from The Elements."

"So, you know about The Community and the life we live?"

"You're from Super Terram?" It was one of the little boys, eyes wide, fork suspended between his plate and his mouth.

"Super Terram? Well, if that means up there. I am." Anne said.

I wasn't sure if I should say I was from the Estates. I didn't know how much we should share with them. Quickly deciding to tell the truth.

"I'm from the Tyson Estate."

"You're from Dome City?" the other boy asked just

as enthralled as his brother.

It was interesting to hear their terminology. I was thoroughly fascinated by them and wanted to learn more.

"Yes, I am."

The two young boys looked wide-eyed at us.

"I'm sure you have a lot of questions, as do we. But first, let's enjoy some dinner, and then Mary Elizabeth will fix you a place to sleep for the night. Tomorrow we will bring you out to see the rest of Sub Terra and find you a Dwelling of your own."

Anne looked at me. I could see concern and confusion in her eyes. I didn't quite know what to make of everything either.

The food was rich and salty. It was all delicious. Nothing like what we ate in the Tyson Estate. More like the food in the Taxter Estate. But far less fancy.

"We don't want to be any trouble."

"Nonsense! We have plenty of room. We are not a vast community of people, we have enough for everyone."

"How is it we have not interacted before?" I asked.

"Well, we have extremely strict rules in Sub Terra, these rules have kept us safe and thriving. Although Abraham Mulcahey has long since left his earthly body, his spirit lives on in his descendants and all of us who follow his gospels."

*Gospels*, I thought to myself. He continued.

"Jessup Mulcahey is our current Pastor. You'll meet him too. He is a direct descendant of Abraham. You'll soon see why we have never had a need for anything but what we have here. That's why we have never ventured to Super Terram or into Dome City."

I wanted to know where they got their electricity, where their food came from. Did they have a communication network down here? How many people lived down here? I suddenly felt very tired, and Anne yawned. Jacob noticed and stood from the table.

"Mary Elizabeth let's get these kids somewhere comfortable. They look exhausted."

"Well, I will set Anne up in the West Room, and Hutch can stay with the boys. It wouldn't be proper to have them stay together."

"We are married, actually," I stated, taking Anne's hand in mine. The thought of being apart from her, after all we had just gone through, worried me.

"What? But you're much too young to be wed!"

"Mary Elizabeth, we are in no position to judge. Can't you see she's with child?"

A look of disapproval crossed the woman's face.

Anne frowned.

"If it would make you more comfortable for us to sleep separately…" I hoped they wouldn't ask us to.

"Nonsense. Mary Elizabeth, please set them up together in the West Room. No more talk about it they're exhausted."

We followed her down a long stone hallway; it was more like a tunnel than a hallway.  The floor was carpeted. Small sconces embedded in the white walls came every 4 feet or so.

We passed a few doors, including the one we had emerged from a little while before, and were led to the very last door.

17

"You should find everything you need in there."
Mary Elizabeth said curtly and turned away from us
walking back down the long hallway.

## **Chapter 2**

I watched Anne sleeping peacefully. Though exhausted, I couldn't sleep. I found myself remembering the events of the past year. My life used to be simple. Boring, but simple. I knew what was expected of me.

I remembered seeing Anne's picture for the first time. My father gave it to me. I didn't know why at the time. When he first asked me to be involved in The Savior Project, I was thrilled to have the opportunity to work with him. In actuality, we didn't spend any additional time together at all. I was instructed to study the subjects. Study their eating habits, sleep patterns, any skills they displayed. Basically, any and all things I could observe and report back on.

Excited for it to be my first assignment, my reports were very thorough.

I watched hours and hours of footage on Anne and Margaret. I used what I learned to design their Domicile. To create their meal boxes. To try and make them feel comfortable.

The more I learned about Anne, the more I cared about what happened to her. I suspected now; it was by design. They wanted me to fall in love with her, so they could orchestrate the creation of a new being, a better being to study.

And now, here we were in a world that didn't make any sense.

I didn't know when it happened, but I did finally fall asleep.

* * * * *

There was Uncle Joe's bat. I knew what I had to do. Before I could think, it was over. I continued striking him, even after he stopped moving. Malakai was dead. I killed him. Killed him for hurting Anne and hurting Maggie. I killed him because I had to, or he would have killed all of us.  Now, I was the murderer. I dropped the bat, feeling nauseous. I looked around Anne's Domicile.  Everything was red. I heard screams. I felt cold. The room seemed to be getting larger. The walls crumbled away. I ran to Anne, but the floor was crumbling beneath her. I reached out to her. I grabbed hold of her hand. It was slick with blood. I couldn't hold her. She was slipping. I held on with all the strength I had left. I felt a tap on my shoulder, relieved someone could help. I looked up to see the mangled face of Malakai, his jaw twisted in an unnatural way. His left eyeball hanging from the socket from a pulsating vein. He gripped my shoulder tight, and I let go of Anne's hand.

"Anne!" I woke up screaming, reaching my arms out in front of me. I didn't recognize where I was.

"Hutch, it's okay. You're okay, I'm here." It was Anne, she was holding me, stroking my hair.

I hugged her, holding on tightly, afraid to fall back into my nightmare.

"Is it morning?" I asked, disoriented.

"I think so. I don't know how they can tell down here."

Anne looked at me with concern in her eyes. "Are you alright?"

"Yes, yes, I'm fine. Just a dream, a really horrible dream."

"Hutch, I'm scared."

I nodded. There was still so much we needed to learn about where we were.

The smell of breakfast drifted into our room. Our

comfortable bed had many pillows, handmade afghans, and soft supple sheets. There were no windows; the only light source was a glowing orb on a table, next to the bed. There was a small dresser, and a rocking chair in the corner. The walls were smooth, made of stone or concrete. On the floor lay an oval-shaped, hand-woven rug.  Everything smelled of earth. I didn't remember changing, but both Anne and I wore soft linen sleeping clothes. A gown for Anne, a shirt and pants for me.

"Are you two awake?" It was Mary Elizabeth knocking on our door.

"Yes, we are awake," I called back to her.

"There are clothes in the top drawer for Hutch, and in the second drawer for Anne. When you're ready, please join us for breakfast."

"Okay, thank you!" I called back to her, quickly

getting out of the bed.

"Hutch, what are we doing? Are we going to stay down here?"

Anne was whispering, holding my hand.

"I don't know yet. Let's go have some breakfast and see what Jacob has to say. We will ask our questions and figure out what to do then."

She nodded. We got up and changed, as Mary Elizabeth directed. The clothes were simple, comfortable. We turned away from each other to change. Anne was in a dress again, which I knew she hated.  She told me once it was because it made her feel weak. She didn't feel she could fight in a dress. The colors were muted and plain. The entire space looked muted and plain.

We made our way to the kitchen. There was no difference in lighting than there had been the night

24

before. A yellow hue enveloped everything.

"Good morning, you two!" Jacob stood at the table; arms spread wide to welcome us. "Sit, sit down. Hope you're hungry!  Did you sleep alright?"

We nodded.  Anne was understandably suspicious. I was too. The food smells helped melt my suspicion slightly.

"May I ask where you get your food from?"

"The Mercatus, silly." It was Caleb. "Where do you get yours from?"

"Caleb, mind your manners. Hutch and Anne are our guests. They are not familiar with our ways."

"The Mercatus?" Anne finally spoke.

"It's our market, where we get all of our food, clothing, and supplies. We will take you there. First, we will need to find you your own Dwelling."

"Why are you being so nice to us?"

"Anne, I know Super Terram is a hostile place to live. Here, in Sub Terra, we live in peace and harmony, with love and God. Welcoming those in need is just our way." Jacob took Anne's hand, and she pulled it away.

"Anne." I was surprised at her reaction.

"It's alright Hutch. I understand. Trust is not something that would come easy from a Super Terran. Down here, we all have faith. Faith in each other, and in all of God's children."

I smiled, truly unsure what to make of them. He spoke like a preacher.

We ate and Jacob talked about what their lives in Sub Terra were like. He didn't ask too many questions about us. Mary Elizabeth didn't speak at all until we were almost finished.

"How far along are you?" she asked, not looking at Anne.

"Just about five months," Anne answered, also not looking up.

"And you're how old?"

"I'm seventeen."

"And him? How old is he?"

"I'm eighteen."

"And when did you get married?"

"Yesterday." Anne's voice annoyed.

"Hm, I see."

"And what's that supposed to mean?" I could feel

Anne's anger growing.

"Mary Elizabeth, that's enough!" Jacob's voice boomed, echoing off the stone walls.

All eyes went to him except his wife's. Hers went to the floor.

"We are not here to judge your choices."

"We should explain." I wanted to break the growing tension at the table.

"You don't need to. Mary Elizabeth, apologize."

"Really, it's alright," I said shaking my head.

"My apologies to both of you. It's not my place." Mary Elizabeth offered.

An awkward silence fell over the table.

Jacob broke the silence with a loud clap of his hands.

"I will take you to your Dwelling. I know exactly the one that will work for you and your growing family. It's not far from here." He waved his hand dismissively at his family, who jumped into action to clear the table.

Anne and I looked at each other. This was certainly a strange way of life. I wasn't sure how much we should share with them about what truly brought us to their world. I decided to wait and see how everything progressed.

## Chapter 3

"This will be your Dwelling."

We had only walked a short distance from Jacob's Dwelling. We passed many doors I assumed led to others.  On one side of us, doors, and the other had some kind of rail track. It looked similar to the track the monorails I was used to ran on.  We walked down a concrete platform. The ceiling above us was tiled with tracks of fluorescent lighting running the length of it.

"You're just giving this to us?"  Anne's eyes were wide with disbelief.

"It's recently vacated, so I know it's available."

I was certain I didn't want to know what happened to

the recent occupant.

"Go ahead, you can go in and check it out. I'm sure you'll find the space adequate."

We swung the small, unlocked door open and stepped in. It was nice, simple, looked very similar to Jacob's.

There was a small living room and a kitchen, a bathroom and a bedroom with a bed large enough for two people and another empty bedroom.

"We can get you a crib at The Mercatus for this room. You'll be needing that soon."

We left the few things we carried out of the Estate with us on the wooden kitchen table and followed Jacob out.

"Now, it's time to meet Jessup Mulcahey."

We understood him to be what would be equivalent to an Estate Head for me, and an Elder for Anne, though he led the entirety of Sub Terra, not just a section or a family. He was the fifth Mulcahey to lead Sub Terra. Only a direct descendant of Abraham Mulcahey could be in that position. Jessup had three sons and the eldest, Ezra, would take over after Jessup. His other two sons Ethan and Elijah would be next in order. I asked Jacob what would happen if there was a generation without a son. He told us it had never happened. The families always had boys and women would not be allowed to fill the position. I knew that wouldn't sit well with Anne, so I didn't pursue the conversation further.

They were a very backward-thinking community. They seemed to be frozen in a time long before even The Shift. There was no evidence of technology. I didn't see any communication devices of any kind in Jacob's Dwelling or ours in the brief time we had to look around.  It was all very primitive.

Jacob led us to a large door, again, not far from our new Dwelling. The door crept open to reveal a man standing at an altar. His arms spread wide, with his back to us. He was reciting what sounded like the sermons I heard when my mother used to take me to church in The Bloch Estate.

"Father, forgive the intrusion, there are some people I would like you to meet."

Jessup spun around. I saw a flash of anger on his face. It disappeared as quickly as I had seen it. So fast, I was unsure if it hadn't been my imagination.

"Welcome, welcome my children."

Anne seemed unfazed. We walked down the aisle to meet him. He greeted us both with firm handshakes. He didn't wear a priest's garb as I had expected. He was in a blue plaid flannel shirt that sat open over a white t-shirt. His pants were tan cotton, and his feet were bare. His hair was long. His face clean-shaven. A large wooden cross hung from a leather rope around his neck. He was tall and imposing in his posture, and even more so when he spoke.

"So, you are here as Jacob's guests. That's wonderful."

He motioned for us to sit down in the front pew of the church.

"Now, why don't you two tell me your story? Everyone has a story and I am guessing you have a good one to share with me, seeing how young you are and that she is with child."

"They are married, Father. Married just yesterday according to them. They are from Super Terram."

"Actually, Anne is from The Community, I am from The Estates."

34

"See, a good story. Do tell."

I looked at Anne, still unsure how much to tell them. Deciding for us, Anne spoke.

"I grew up out in The Elements with my little sister Maggie. Our parents died a long time ago, so we've been on our own for quite some time. About eight months ago we were kidnapped and brought into The Tyson Estate to be studied, because the bubbles are failing and they wanted to see how we were able to live out there, so they could figure out how to live out there when they no longer had the bubbles to protect them. That's where I met Hutch.  He grew up in the Tyson Estate, and was one of the people working in the lab studying us. To make a long story short, they implanted me with an embryo made from me and Hutch to create their next test subject. They also implanted my sister; we were both in comas at the time. My sister is dead and the baby with her."

Anne's eyes moistened.

Jessup and Jacob stood dumbfounded by her story.

"So, this baby, your baby was conceived without sin."

"If you mean not conceived in the traditional sense, then yeah. We got married so we could escape The Estate. We didn't want them to dissect me, Hutch or our baby."

"Extraordinary." Jessup tented his hands and placed them to his chin. "Did you have help?"

"Yes, we had a lot of help. Not everyone in The Estates agrees with The Savior Project. We needed to deactivate the trackers they put on everyone who is part of the project, and the person who had the tech to deactivate them was the preacher who married us. That's why we had to get married so we could get to that Estate before escaping." Anne finished the story and fell silent. She had been through so much in so little time.

"Yes, we landed down here very much accidentally, and really appreciate the hospitality and kindness Jacob has shown us," I added.

"Of course, he has. That is our way."

Jessup sat silent, thoughtful for a long moment. When he finally spoke, he put a hand on one of each of our shoulders.

"I would like to welcome you both to our congregation and look forward to learning more about you. Please come to our next service."

"When is that?" I asked.

"Today at noon."

Anne and I looked at each other, and then to Jacob.

"Yes, of course, I will bring them with us."

37

I had been to a Catholic mass before, but I was certain Anne had only been to church to meet Daryl Tyson, and for our wedding.

"This will give us enough time to get everything they need at The Mercatus and be back here for the noon service."

"Excellent. We will see you then."

Jacob herded us out of the church, to bring us to The Mercatus.

We followed the tracks on our left for a long while, until reaching The Mercatus. The tunnel walls and ceiling were covered with tiles of different colors. We passed signs with street names on them. I thought I could see Anne recognizing a few as we walked. If she did, she didn't say so. Pillars littered our way as well, some with signs with illegible print worn away from time.

The narrow corridor suddenly opened into a vast hall. A grand tiled ceiling above us. It was a flurry of activity. Brightly lit, loud and bustling. We came upon it so suddenly, without warning. It took my breath away. Tents and tables were set up all around, with everything you could possibly be looking for.

Jacob led us straight to a tent selling cribs.

I could feel eyes on us. It was not surprising. We certainly stuck out in their space.

This tent was jam-packed with wooden furniture. Not just cribs but rocking chairs and dressers, side tables and chests. There wasn't much room to get around.

Anne ran her hand over several things, her other hand resting on her belly. Her eyes sparkled as she navigated her way carefully through the city of furniture. She looked so beautiful and relaxed almost. The idea of getting something for Eden calmed her in some way.

"I really like this one." She motioned me over to look at it with her.

It was carefully handcrafted by someone who took great care and attention to detail. Small flowers intricately carved in the head and footboards and across the railings. It was truly stunning.

"That piece is my favorite too." An older man dressed in brown overalls, wearing a long white beard without a mustache, approached us.

"Did you make this?" Anne asked, eyes wide.

"Guilty."

"It's really incredible."

"Thank you, I'm quite proud of it. It's important it goes to a very special baby, and I have a feeling the one you're carrying is pretty special."

I didn't know what to make of him. Was he simply trying to make a sale, or was he being genuine?

"Hello, Barnabas!" Jacob approached with a hearty handshake for the older man.

"Good morning, Jacob! Are these two your guests?"

"Yes, my friend, and anything they want please charge to my Commodum."

"Oh no, we couldn't ask that of you. That's too generous. You've been so kind to us already."

"Nonsense. Hutch, you need to start getting used to the hospitality down here. It's abundant."

"No need, Jacob. It will be gratis from me. This special piece needs to go to this lovely young family. I will have it sent to your Dwelling right away. You'll need a pad, and beddings as well. Naomi, three tents down, she will have what you need. Tell her Barnabas sent you, and I will take care of everything."

I didn't understand their generosity.

Anne and I looked at each other. I was certain she was feeling the same way I was.

"It's too much, really."

"What else are you going to do? You don't have the means to get any of the things yourself. We all help each other here. Someday you will be asked to help, too, and you will remember our generosity, and want to give back. It's how things work down here."

"We will repay you, all of you. I promise."

Anne looked at me. I wasn't sure if she was alright with everything. I desperately wanted to talk to her privately.

Instead, we followed Jacob to Naomi's tent. She seemed to be expecting us.

"Hello, hello! Come in, come in! I have many things for you to choose from!"

Naomi was even older than Barnabas. Her spine was horribly curved. She walked with a cane and wore a crocheted shawl over her hunched back. Her smile revealed a set of yellow decaying teeth, betraying her age and physical imparities. She was as cheerful as she was old.

She ushered us deeper into the tent. Hand sewn tapestries hung from bars above, piles of blankets lined a narrow pathway through her space.

"I have everything you need right back here."

She handed us blankets and sheets and pillows, and a crib pad.  She then handed us teddy bears, and baby clothes, and cloth diapers.

She even gave Anne some dresses that would accommodate her as she got further along in her pregnancy.

She told us everything would be delivered to our Dwelling, then sent us to our next stop for more clothing, this time for both of us.

A young woman, not much older than us, named Esther, had piles of outfits, complete with shoes, ready for us. She assured us we wouldn't have to try them on. We needed only to approve them, and they would be sent to our Dwelling. She wore a dress similar to Anne's. Her skin as pale as everyone else's, her eyes large and bright blue. She was clearly at least a Second Gen Dweller, if not a third or fourth.

Esther directed us to our next stop, which was for groceries. Jacob helped us pick out all of the food we would need. We didn't pay for anything; everything was being sent straight to our Dwelling. So, we left

44

every spot empty-handed.  By the time we were done, I didn't remember half the things we "bought".

Easy. Strange. Suspicious.

## Chapter 4

"Welcome my flock. Welcome to Sunday Mass. In the name of the Father, the Son and the Holy Spirit, amen."

Jessup stood; arms spread in front of the modest altar we had seen earlier that day. The pews were packed with people. Jacob and his family brought us to the very front pew of the church. We sat holding hands, feeling all eyes on us. They were obviously curious about us. I expected Jessup to introduce us and prepared myself for it. I whispered to Anne to expect it as well. She nodded, squeezing my hand tighter.

Jessup continued his sermon. It was long and verbose, and I stopped listening after a while. We rose, and sat, then knelt, and rose and sat again several times. There was singing and chanting. It was really beautiful and very odd to us. I felt how I did when I was cast out into The Elements, and how Anne must have felt when she came to The Estates. Everything so foreign.

"Now, my family, I know you are all curious about the new members of our flock. They are guests of the Hensley Family. Jacob brought them to meet me this morning, and they are a lovely young couple expecting their first child in a few months. Please welcome them as I have, with grace and faith."

He motioned for us to turn and face the rest of the church. A sea of smiling faces stared back at us. They were all extremely interested, and excited to meet us. I knew it was about to get very overwhelming for Anne. She even stepped slightly behind me, feeling the weight of their eyes on her.

"Please feel free to join us downstairs for some

refreshments, provided by the Swanson Family. Thank you, Samuel and Mary Katherine."

Two parishioners stood up and waved.

"Now, go with God, my children."

Everyone filtered to a stairwell behind the altar. I knew we would be expected to join them. I took Anne's hand and started to follow them, but she pulled me back.

"I do not want to go down there," she whispered.

"We have to, Anne. With everything they've done for us, it would be rude to leave."

"Well, then, I feel sick and I want to lay down."

I knew she was lying. I thought that was a bad idea, considering where we were. The look on her face told me she wasn't going down to that basement under any circumstances.

"Okay, stay here, I'll be right back."

Reluctantly, she released my hand. I approached Jessup to explain.

"Hello, Hutch!" He greeted me with a strong handshake and a slap on the shoulder.

"Hello, sir."

"Please, call me Father."

"Yes, of course, Father, Anne is not feeling well, nausea, I think I should get her back to our Dwelling to get settled."

"A lot of people are looking forward to meeting you downstairs." He motioned to the stairwell leading to the basement. His tone was tense. His grip on my shoulder tightening.

"I know, but she is really not doing well, and I want to make sure she and the baby are alright, above all else."

I shook my shoulder from his hand and turned to walk away.

"Of course, of course. We will see you at the next mass then."

"When is that?" I asked turning back.

"Tomorrow morning at 9:30 AM."

"How often do you hold service?"

"Three times a day Monday through Saturday and twice on Sunday."

"Does everyone come to all of them?" I couldn't imagine it.

"No, of course not, we want to make sure we give our

congregation as many opportunities as possible."

"Oh, I see."

"So, I hope she feels better, and we'll see you tomorrow."

The way he said it sounded more like a command than a request. I didn't feel the need to explore the conversation any further, knowing Anne wanted to leave.

I rejoined her, and we exited the church away from all the people, who would undoubtedly be extremely disappointed we would not be joining them.

I nodded to Jacob, who looked confused.

"Where are you going?"

"We're going back to our Dwelling. Anne isn't feeling well."

"Oh, okay."

"Thank you, Jacob, for everything. I hope we will be able to return the hospitality you've shown us."

"Oh, you will. I'm sure of it." I was taken aback by how he said it. There was something ominous in his voice. "Do you know how to get back?"

"Yes, we'll manage. Thanks again."

We walked back the way I remembered Jacob taking us. Following the tracks, now on our right. I meant to ask if trains still ran but assumed, they didn't since everyone seemed to walk everywhere.

The walk back felt longer, and I was worried I had passed our place. I was about to backtrack when I recognized where we were.

The outside wall to our Dwelling was covered in shiny cream and dark green colored tiles, forming an intricate and beautiful design framing the arched doorway.  A sign next to it said Chambers Street. The tiles were shiny, and smooth to the touch. All the walls were lined with tiles, many dull, broken and cracked with age.  I wasn't clear what the purpose of the space was before the Shift. I assumed an underground railway of sorts. We hadn't come across a way to get above ground, only passages and stairwells leading throughout, or further down.

When we reached the wooden door to our Dwelling, I noticed it was slightly ajar.  I could see shadows.

"Anne, there's someone in there. Wait here."

Anne stayed back as I approached.

"Hello? Who's there?"

"It's alright, my name is Jeremiah, I am delivering the items from The Mercatus."

"How did you get in here?"

"Oh, well, nobody locks their doors in Sub Terra."

"Why bother having locks then?" I asked, annoyed they felt it alright to come and go as they pleased in other people's houses.

"Well, when we're home we use them. It's just when we're out we leave the doors open in case anyone needs to get in like to deliver something. I was asked to set your home up while you were at mass. You weren't supposed to be back so soon."

He sounded sincere.

I waved to Anne to come in, and she joined us inside.

"My apologies, miss."

"Anne this is Jeremiah. He was delivering all the items from the market today."

Anne nodded, and without a word disappeared into the bedroom.

"Thank you, Jeremiah, we can take it from here."

The young man bowed awkwardly and left.

All of our cupboards were now full. I opened the refrigerator, full. I checked all the cabinets and drawers. We were fully stocked and outfitted. Glassware, dinnerware, utensils, all there and neatly put away. The bathroom was the same. I couldn't remember what had been there when Jacob brought us the first time. Was everything new, or had some things already been there?

I walked into the baby's room. It was set up almost like a shrine. It was unnerving. There were unlit candles decorating each side of the crib, with a painting of Mother Mary, holding baby Jesus in her arms above it. There was a similar painting in the church in The Bloch Estate. The crib Anne had chosen sat complete with the pillows and blankets we chose with Naomi. It was astonishing to me; all of it was done in such a short amount of time. It certainly couldn't have been Jeremiah alone to set the space up. I remembered setting Anne and Maggie's Domicile up. It took months to create.

I found Anne laying on the bed in the bedroom. She was sleeping. She looked peaceful. I placed a blanket over her and left her alone, heading back out to the living area. My stomach growled, reminding me we hadn't eaten in several hours. I decided to explore our stocked fridge.

I found some sliced meat and cheese. Hand kneaded baked bread from the bread box on the counter. I wasn't sure if it was simply hunger, but it all tasted very good.

Looking around, I tried to figure out where the

electricity ran from. There were outlets throughout, and the main light in the center of the ceiling was wired into the fixture. The plumbing seemed normal. Not surprising, it was all one level. What was surprising was the temperature. It was comfortable. There were cooler spots and warmer spots. Not one extreme or the other. It was all extraordinary to me. I still couldn't believe we never knew about an entire society of people, living right below us.

"Hutch, I'm hungry."

Anne came out of the bedroom.

"I can make you a sandwich." I offered cheerfully.

She nodded, and I made her the same sandwich I ate.

She seemed to like it, smiling at me. "Thank you."

"You're welcome."

"What do you think of all this?" she asked, between bites.

"Honestly, I don't know what to think."

"They seem way too nice."

"I agree. I can't imagine this is just how they are all the time."

"Hutch, there's no such thing as a perfect peaceful society. These people are so nice it's creepy. And Jessup, what about him?"

"I don't know. I think you're rubbing off on me, Anne, I don't trust anything anymore."

When she finished eating, she joined me, snuggling up next to me on our couch.

"I guess this is just what we have to get used to, at least until the baby's born."

"I do think that's best, Anne, I don't want to risk you having Eden out in The Elements. It's too unpredictable."

"I do agree with you, Hutch. It would be easier to have her down here, where it's at least warm."

She took my hand and pulled my arm around her tighter.

"I love you, Hutch. I will do whatever you want." She looked up at me with her big blue eyes. "Just promise me you'll never leave me, no matter what happens."

"I promise."

## Chapter 5

"Uncle Joe?"

Anne ran ahead of me, to a man I didn't recognize, but I knew from her stories of him. It was our first venture out since we settled into our Dwelling in Sub Terra, what we still called The Underground.

"Annie?"

He recognized her immediately. They embraced warmly. Turning to me with smiles, I felt their eyes on me, and I suddenly felt uncomfortable.

"This is Hutch, my husband."

"Husband? What? I can't believe you're old enough to be married!"

He shook my hand firmly. Almost too firmly.

"It's kind of a long story." I watched Anne regale basically her whole life to her long-lost friend.

I sat, quietly listening as they caught up.

I wasn't entirely sold on whether or not Joe was a friendly, or if I should be suspicious of his motives.

He took us around the market and introduced us to more of the Sub Terra Dwellers.

He welcomed us into his home, where we met his wife Magda, and children Matthew and Joe Jr.

Their space was similar to the accommodations we were given. I was still unclear why everyone was so nice. I am not normally a cynic, but I found my head crammed with negative thoughts I couldn't shake.

Anne wouldn't understand. I was the one who

pushed for us to journey down here. I insisted we stay until the baby was born. I was beginning to second guess our decision.

Sub Terra and its Dwellers were turning out to be more of a mystery the more we learned.

Uncle Joe seemed to sense my uneasiness as we sat on an overstuffed, plaid couch in his Dwelling. Anne sat in an equally overstuffed chair across from us. He put an arm around me and patted my shoulder. He wore the long dark beard Anne had described to me although there was a lot of gray and white mixed in. His eyes were kind, as was his smile. His face, lined with age, made him look wise. I could understand why Anne cared for him so much.

"Don't worry, Hutch. We're all genuinely good people down here. We live peacefully. Really."

"How did you end up down here, Uncle Joe?" Anne looked and sounded relaxed. More so than I had ever seen her.

"Exactly like you did. I was out scouting for a pull and fell down a hole. I became the guest of Magda's family. Her parents took me in, confused and cold, covered in all those layers we were so used to. My welcome to Sub Terra was similar to yours, which is why I know exactly what you're feeling, Hutch. I was as skeptical about their good intentions as I am sensing you are. You'll discover quickly that we are all on the same side, just trying to survive in the Post Shift world."

"Did you ever try to go back up there?" I asked, still not convinced, despite his kind eyes and smile.

"No, it was a choice I made when I came down here. And a choice you'll have to make as well. Leaving Sub Terra is strictly forbidden. It's how we stay invisible,

63

and how we stay safe."

"So, we get to choose if we stay or not?" Anne looked down at Eden in her belly.

"Yes, Annie, you have until your Exordium to decide."

"Exordium?"

"It's your introduction to the flock, as Jessup would call it. It's when you surrender your loyalties and faith to Jessup and the rest of the parish and become one of us. You will swear loyalty and faith to our church."

"How long before that happens?"

"Well, it's a big deal, so there are preparations and Jessup had to approve you first, which he has. I'm sure they've already begun planning."

"What if we refuse?"

"That is your choice, Hutch. No one has ever refused so I honestly don't know what they would do."

"Do you want to leave, Hutch? I thought you wanted me to have the baby here. I thought you said it would be safer for her and for me if we had her here. We're here because you said we should stay, I listened to you." I could see tears brimming in her eyes, and it broke my heart.

"I did, I do. I just want information, that's all." I got up to meet Anne, who was standing then. I took her hands in mine, "I still think we should stay here to have Eden. It's for the best."

"Well, that's great!" Uncle Joe also rose, "Magda, let's get some lunch ready."

I squeezed Anne's hand, and smiled at her. She smiled weakly back at me, wiping her tears before they could roll down her cheeks.

"Come now, let's eat."

We followed Uncle Joe to his dining room for a thoroughly enjoyable lunch. They shared stories of their time out in The Elements, laughing at their memories. Magda, who didn't look much older than us, seemed disinterested in hearing about her husband's life before. Anne enjoyed every moment. It was nice to hear her laugh, to see her remember good times in her life. Uncle Joe took her parents' place for her after they died. He was as important to her as my parents were to me. She was thriving on the pride he showed in her. I loved seeing her like that.

Magda noticed it too.

"Well, it's a good thing you got away from that awful place." She interrupted.

"It wasn't all awful. We really didn't know any other

way. It was our life back then." Uncle Joe defended their life out there.

"It all sounds terrible. The way you lived; it sounds like the worst place in the world. You should be thankful we took you in, Joseph. You two should be grateful to Jacob and his family. Now, I don't want to hear any more about life out in The Elements. This is your home now and the sooner you start embracing it, the better you will be. Excuse me, I need to check on the children." She stood and walked out of the dining room, without looking back.

If she had looked back, she would have seen the dumbfounded look on our faces.

"Don't mind her. She's not a fan of me having had a life before meeting her." Uncle Joe leaned in whispering to us.

"I'm actually getting a little tired, Hutch, can we go

home?  Thank you so much for lunch and a wonderful morning."

I rose to help Anne with her chair, adding, "Please tell Magda goodbye and thank you from us."

"Of course," Uncle Joe rose too, and walked us to the door.

"We'll see you at mass tomorrow morning.  They will want to speak to you about The Exordium and your intentions."

Anne and I nodded and left.  As soon as we were out of earshot Anne spoke, "I don't think she liked me very much."

"She's jealous, Anne."

"Of me?  That's ridiculous."

"Not of you, well, not entirely.  She's jealous that you

knew Uncle Joe before she did."

"He's like a father to me."

"Yes, of course. She just doesn't share those memories with him as you do, and it probably made her feel left out."

"Well, that's silly. I wouldn't care if someone told me they knew you before me. Are you jealous of Uncle Joe?"

"A little, maybe. You are so comfortable with him. More so than you are with me."

"Well, now you're being silly. I love you and I am completely comfortable with you."

We walked following the tracks, holding hands. There never seemed to be anyone else walking where we were. It was strange. We hadn't seen much of the underground. Only our corridor, and as far as The

Mercatus. I saw tunnels leading in another direction from The Mercatus; they were labeled with track numbers. I assumed it led to the other Dwellings. I hadn't seen anyone coming or going from the other doorways we saw in our corridor, and it was always painfully quiet. I wasn't sure anyone lived in them. Jacob's Dwelling was close by. I wasn't sure exactly which one anymore. It was similar to The Combine in that way. I knew what direction we were going in based on the tracks. I didn't know how far they went. I didn't know how far our corridor went. I wasn't anxious to explore anything either. Anne didn't appear curious at all. She wanted to stay in our Dwelling all the time. It had taken some convincing to get her to go back to The Mercatus. Then we saw Uncle Joe, and she was clearly happy we had gone.

So then there was Uncle Joe. The big mystery of what had happened to him was solved. He fell down a hole like we did and stayed to marry the daughter of the family whose Dwelling he fell into. I should have asked how often people from The Community fell down holes into Sub Terra. None of it sat well with me. I couldn't shake the uneasiness. At the same time, all I wanted was for Anne and Eden to be safe. If it meant dealing with the oddities of Sub Terra, I was willing to do that.

## Chapter 6

After meeting with Jessup about our intention to stay, the day of our Exordium was set for the following month. It was a rather large to do. I felt like we were planning another wedding. All of Sub Terra would be there, and it would take place at The Mercatus. All the shops would shut down for the celebration.

The actual Exordium ceremony would happen at the church, with only Jessup, Jacob's family as our hosts and Anne had asked if Uncle Joe could attend as well, which with some reluctance was eventually allowed.

We were given ceremonial garb to wear; they were long collarless, long-sleeved, linen gowns. Crosses identical to the one Jessup wore, and crowns made of dried flowers, vines, and branches. They were delivered in a small wooden trunk the day before.

"This is weird."  Anne spoke first, as we opened and looked through the trunk.

"Yeah, it is."

It all seemed too ritualistic to be of the Catholic traditions I learned about and followed when my mother was alive.  I didn't remember everything, but I certainly never saw anything like this. The way Jessup described the ceremony sounded very much like a baptism.  I had seen one when I was only seven. I remember it being a happy occasion for the parents holding the baby. I asked my mother what it all meant, and it was a nice story.

What we were about to go through didn't sound nice.  It felt like we were signing our souls away. It felt like a cult.  I had heard rumors of one that formed in The Winchester Estate once. There were stories of a secret society of people performing animal sacrifices and reading from a book they called a Grimoire. It was supposed to contain magic or some other nonsense.

This Exordium felt more like that than anything truly religious or God-like. In the days since we fell into Sub Terra, nothing helped to ease my mind about what we had gotten ourselves into. I only hoped we could keep to ourselves until the baby was born, and then decide what to do next. The idea of raising a new baby out in The Elements was the furthest from what I wanted for us. We didn't have many choices. We could try to go back to The Estates, maybe a different one, not Tyson. Maybe Daryl Tyson could hide us in The Bloch Estate. He was so willing to help us get out. I felt bad, we were unable to reach Tiny to let him know we were safe. I didn't bring it up to Anne. We could wait to discuss everything until after Eden was born. For now, we simply needed to survive

The Exordium, and figure out our part in Sub Terra.

Lost in thought, I didn't realize I had been holding the cross in my hand the entire time.  Anne took it from me with a look of concern.

"You okay?" she asked, dropping the necklace into the trunk.  It made a hollow knocking sound as it hit the bottom.

"Yes, I'm fine.  How are you feeling?"

"Freaked out about all of this.  I keep thinking of it the way I thought about the wedding.  A means to an end. We are here for the duration until Eden is here and likely for a while after.  But not forever, right?"

"Oh, definitely not forever.  These people are crazy."

"Oh, I'm so glad to hear you say that."

She ran to me and wrapped her arms around my

neck.  We kissed. We hadn't done much of that in a while. It was nice.  She kept kissing me. I was surprised.

"Anne, what are you doing?"

"Kissing my husband."  She giggled and ran into the bedroom.

I wasn't sure if I should follow her.  Then, there was a knock at our door.

"Hutch, Miss Anne, it's Jeremiah.  Jessup asked if you both could come to the church, right away."

What could he possibly want now?  This complete involvement in our lives was already getting tiring.

"Anne, we have to go."

"What?  Where?" She sounded as annoyed as I felt.

"Jessup wants to see us at the church."

"What for?"

"He has some stuff to go over before tomorrow," Jeremiah answered from the doorway.

I didn't let him in, despite his attempts to walk past me. I was attempting to teach boundaries. I didn't care how they lived. I had my limits, as did Anne.

We joined Jeremiah and followed him to the church. Jessup was there, waiting for us at the altar. Jeremiah ran up to him and said something in a hushed voice. I couldn't hear what they were saying.

"Thank you for coming." He looked serious, "I wanted to speak to you both before tomorrow. I need you to understand what you're committing to. Once you become a member of our family, you become part of the circuitry that keeps Sub Terra alive. We expect you to find your place quickly, to see what you bring to the table. You have expressed the want to repay those of us who have shown our generosity to you, and I believe the opportunity to do so could happen soon."

I couldn't imagine what he could mean by that. I just nodded in response. Anne mimicked me.

"Good.  Here in Sub Terra, we have sacrificed a great deal to stay invisible to Super Terram and the Dome City.  We don't want any part of their worlds. We have everything we need down here. I know your intention is to live amongst us as one of us.  With your backgrounds being from both Super Terram and Dome City, I have concerns. I need to be sure it is truly your intention to stay, and not to leave us once your child is born."

Did they have cameras or microphones in our Dwelling?  How could he have known? They lacked the tech down here, as far as I saw.

Anne spoke first, taking Jessup's hand, "Father, it is our full intention and our honor to become a part of the Sub Terra family.  We are blessed to have stumbled into your world. I believe it was God's intention to bring us here and to you."

I looked at her astonished.  She looked sincere. I didn't say a word.

"Anne, that is well said.  I do believe you were meant to be here with us.  I am thrilled you have embraced the presence of God in your place with us."

She took his hand and placed it on her stomach. "Eden. That is the name we have chosen for our baby.  Eden, like paradise. Like what we've found here with you and our new family."

Was she acting?  She had to be. She was incredibly convincing. Even I believed her.

"Eden." Jessup raised his hand, saying her name with

purpose. "That is truly beautiful. I have heard enough. We will see you *three* tomorrow."

I never spoke. We left the church and walked in silence back to our Dwelling.

When we got there Anne got a piece of paper and started scribbling on it. She slid it to me.

*I think they have spies or are somehow hearing us in here.*

I wrote back.

*Yes, I think so too.*

We started to search the living room and kitchen for anything that resembled a camera or microphone. Climbing on furniture, moving anything not attached, while being careful not to draw any attention to anyone who might be listening or watching.

Nothing.

We searched the bedroom and bathroom.

Still nothing.

Then I saw it. A small vent in the far wall opposite the front door. It was low, close to the floor. It didn't seem like much. I hadn't noticed it before. I snapped my fingers to get Anne's attention and pointed at it.

She was quick to my side. There was no sign of a microphone. I had to lie down on the floor to see it more closely. The vent covered what looked like a small, long, narrow pipeline. I couldn't see how far it ran. I remembered bringing a flashlight with us the night we escaped The Tyson Estate. I ran to find it. Anne wrote something else on her piece of paper.

*We should talk normally, or they are going to think something is up.*

"I'm getting a little tired. I think I'm going to lay down."

"Okay, Anne, I am going to stay here and read for a little while." I thought it was smart to say we were doing things that would explain extended silence.

Finding my flashlight in a drawer in the kitchen, I shined it through the vent. I could see the pipe. It ran further than my light could reach. I quickly faced the light away; afraid someone might see it on the other end. This had to be how they were hearing what we said. They may not be able to hear everything, but they heard enough for us to get called to see Jessup.

Just as I was about to get up, I heard voices coming from the vent. I guessed the sound traveled both ways. It was slightly muffled. I could make out what they were saying, if I didn't move or even breathe.

Anne moved towards me; the sound of her footsteps

was so loud as I strained to hear the voices. I put a hand up to stop her, then a finger to my mouth. I pointed to the vent and made a talking sign with my hand and pointed to my ear. She stopped moving.

"You told me you heard them say something about leaving." It was an extremely upset Jessup.

"Yes, Father. That's what I thought I heard." Jeremiah's voice was clear. He sounded terrified.

The sound of a slap followed.

"I'm sorry, Father."

"Get out, I don't want to see your face anymore."

"What did he think he heard?" It was Jacob this time.

"It doesn't matter. Did you hear her? You can't fake that kind of surrender. The boy, I don't know if he has, but he will do whatever she wants. That I am sure of."

"So, then we're alright?  My family will still get credit?"

"Yes, Jacob, of course.  They are your guests.  You will, of course, get credit."

Get credit?  Credit for what?  What could they be talking about?

"Okay, good. My family is very excited to have the honor this year."

"This year will be extra special, Jacob.  Let's not talk here. We will plan further after The Exordium tomorrow.  There is much to plan before that child is born."

"Eden, what a fitting name they've chosen."

"Jeremiah, can I trust you to take your post and

actually report what you hear, not what you think you hear?"

"Yes, Father. I will not fail you again."

"Don't forget to check the other spot too, in case they're talking in the bedroom."

I listened further, but there was nothing left to hear.

Getting up from the floor quietly, I went into the bedroom to find the other vent. Anne followed me in. She had her paper in hand.

*What did you hear?*

I didn't answer as I found the other vent behind the bed frame. We went into the baby's room to see if there was one in there too. There wasn't. I felt comfortable speaking at a low volume. The sound clearly carried better in the other direction.

I recapped what I heard for Anne.

"What does that mean?" she whispered.

"I don't know," I answered, shaking my head.

"So, they're planning something for us? For the baby? But Uncle Joe. Why would he lie to us?"

"Anne, he may not be the man he was when you knew him."

She didn't like that answer.

"So, now we have to watch what we say in the bedroom and the living room," I said taking her hand to lead her out of the baby's room.

"It's just like in the Domicile. Someday I would like to live a simple life with you, Hutch."

She smiled, shaking her head.

We walked out into the living room.

"Are you coming to bed?" Anne asked nonchalantly.

"Yes, I'll be there shortly, just finishing a chapter." I was getting better at lying. Anne seemed so good at it I was afraid I wouldn't know when she was lying to me. I hoped she would never need to.

I went around and closed the shutters. We had two windows. One next to the door and one in the bedroom. There was a small opening high in the wall between the bedroom and the baby's room. I hoped it wasn't enough to let the sound travel to the vent. It was unlikely.

After I felt our Dwelling was secure, I met Anne in the bedroom. She was already asleep. I was quick to follow. Tomorrow would be a long day.

## Chapter 7

Anne and I woke, and dressed in our ceremonial gowns, placed the wooden crosses around our neck and the crowns on our heads.  We looked and felt ridiculous. We spoke briefly in Eden's room about how we would act for the day. We planned to fully embrace the experience and "surrender". as Jessup called it, and the way Anne had expressed the evening before.  I was certain it was going to be exceedingly difficult for me. Anne seemed excited to pull it off.

We also planned a signal if either of us was ready to leave before the party ended.  Anne would simply feign fatigue and nausea if she was ready to go. I would ask her how she was feeling if I wanted to leave.

With the plan set, I opened the shutters to our windows. Anne and I stepped out of our front door. We were met by a crowd of people. All there to escort us to the church, despite not being allowed in for the ceremony.

Holding hands and smiling widely for the crowd, we made our way to the church. I caught sight of Jeremiah. He had a bruise on his left cheek, where I assumed Jessup had hit him. I felt bad for him. I knew it wasn't his idea to spy on us.

I wondered what I would be asked to do. What they would expect from us following The Exordium. I knew they wouldn't expect Anne to work. They would then expect me to work for two. We would have to figure out a way to support ourselves and find a way to pay back everyone who helped us get settled.

Uncle Joe waited for us at the front door of the

90

church with a bright smile. "Are you excited?"

"Sure, something like that," I answered.

The ceremony was much shorter than I expected. We repeated what Jessup asked us to, vowing loyalty and faith to Sub Terra, and our new brothers and sisters. We promised to live and act as they do and contribute to the success and longevity of our new family.

We were instructed to kneel in front of the altar. Jessup dipped his hand into a large vat of water and drew the sign of the cross on our foreheads. I felt the cool water drip down the front of my face. A drop ran over my right eye and clung to my eyelashes. I looked to my left to see Anne. I know it was the water in my eyes, but I could swear I saw her glow. I looked up, and it distorted the image of Jessup above me. I blinked and it ran down my cheek.

He motioned for us to rise, smiled broadly and said, "Welcome to our family."

There was weak applause from the few people in attendance. We turned to face them, wiping dry our faces as if we were crying.

Uncle Joe and Jacob escorted us out to meet the crowd. They cheered loudly as we exited the church in celebration. The men shook our hands, and the women kissed our cheeks, welcoming us into their world. It was totally bizarre, and we hated every second of it. Still, we went along and acted as if this was the greatest day of our lives. Anne was doing a great job. Me, not so much. I didn't like everyone touching us. Putting their hands-on Anne's stomach. The women all had suggestions for Anne from how to burp the baby to how to get her to sleep through the night.

I kept getting slapped on the back. I didn't appreciate

it. I couldn't wait to get all of it over with.  We finally got to The Mercatus and the celebration started immediately.  Music played, people danced, children squealed loudly, being playfully chased by an oddly dressed clown.  The sound of everything echoing, bouncing off the tiled walls and ceilings.

A table set up on a platform was meant for us.  Anne was right, it felt reminiscent of our wedding.  It was impossible to believe that was only a few weeks before.  We thought our lives had changed so much then. Now, it was unrecognizable.

Anne smiled and played along.   I attempted to do the same, with some success. I felt like we just signed our souls away, and now were celebrating it.

Jessup gave a blessing before we could eat.  The food was good at least. And there was a lot of it.  I still didn't understand where they got their food from. Anne and I had not seen past The Mercatus. The source had to be somewhere beyond the tents down other tunnels. I hoped now, as part of the flock, we would be able to access more information.

Jessup asked us to stand. We did and the group in front of us cheered gleefully. I didn't even hear anything he said. It was a total role reversal from being in The Tyson Estate. Anne seemed to embrace what was happening to us here, while I resisted.

She took my hand and gave it a squeeze.

"You okay?" she asked, still smiling, speaking from the side of her mouth.

I nodded and smiled, widely betraying how I was feeling.

"Now, let us feast and celebrate our new brother, sister and their blessed child on the way."

Glasses were raised. Anne and I followed suit.

94

Finally, we sat to eat, without interruption. No one came up to us, no one asked us questions, no one touched us. I welcomed the respite.

Anne stood without being prompted. She tapped her glass the way Tiny had instructed me to do at our wedding reception to get everyone's attention.

"Hello, my brothers and sisters. I am so proud to call you all that now. I want to thank you all for your kindness and generosity. Hutch and I feel so blessed and welcome here in Sub Terra. We are very much looking forward to meeting all of you and sharing our lives with you. Especially that of our daughter's when she gets here. Sadly, I have to excuse us. I am feeling very tired. It's been a long day and this little one takes a lot out of me." She motioned to her growing belly.

There were sighs of disappointment, with murmurs of understanding.

Jessup stood up, surprised, likely not used to anyone else dictating when something was over.

"Yes, of course." He said standing, recovering from his initial shock at Anne's announcement.

"Please feel free to continue the festivities without us. And thank you all again so much for your wealth of kindness and charity. God bless."

Anne stepped away from our table, holding her hand out to me. I could see Jessup's face as he watched us leave. I wasn't sure if it was a look of disdain or pride. He was clearly fond of Anne, and maybe even admired what she'd done. Or, he was insanely angry. Either way, I was happy to be leaving, and loved Anne even more. We walked off the platform and headed back to our Dwelling.

## Chapter 8

### *ABIGAIL 25033*

I remember that night so vividly.  Sitting in the corner of Maggie's operatory, missing my friend. I started to get up to leave when Annie and Hutch rushed in. I thought everyone, including them, was at their wedding celebration.

I watched as Annie kissed Maggie's cheek, whispered something, then went to the wall. She yanked the plug from the outlet. I was about to get up to protest when they both ran swiftly out the door. What was she doing? She was killing Maggie, why?

They disappeared out the door and before I could get to Maggie. An unbearably loud alarm sounded. Maggie was suddenly surrounded by a team of coats.

"Get Dr. Kelly, now!" One of them screamed.

They were working to get the machines on again.

Maggie lay there, dying or dead, I wasn't sure.

Then with a loud gasp of air, she sat up.

I stayed in my corner, hiding out of sight and watched as they all stood stunned, she had woken up. They all seemed at a loss of what to do. Maggie coughed pulling a tube from her throat, looking around, confused. One of the coats began examining her.

"Where am I?" she asked, her voice raspy.

"Margaret, please lay back. We're getting Dr. Kelly."

"Where's Annie?"

"Just please, lay back."

I didn't know what to do. I was thrilled to see my friend awake. Tears sprang to my eyes. I didn't dare move from my hiding spot. Dr. Kelly entered the room, with a look of astonishment and concern.

"What happened? What are her vitals? The 2GC?"

"The machines are all down. We're trying to get them back up."

"Maggie, it's Dr. Kelly, do you know where you are?"

"In the combine?" Her voice was soft.

"Yes, good." Dr. Kelly's voice relaxed slightly.

"Where's Annie?" Maggie searched the room.

"Somebody get Dr. Sanford in here, right away." Dr. Kelly ordered firmly.

There was a flurry of movement. I stayed where I was, afraid they would think I had something to do with it.

"Somebody turn these damn alarms off!" Dr. Kelly's agitation grew.

"The machines are back up." One of the Coats announced.

Another flurry of movement.

"Where is Annie!?" Maggie shouted, silencing everyone.

"Maggie, we don't know. We are trying to get you back online, so we can make sure you're alright." Dr. Kelly was quick to her side, panic audible in her voice.

What was happening? I shifted and clumsily pushed the table I was hiding behind. It screeched loudly, metal on metal.

"Who's there? Come out, immediately and show yourself." Dr. Kelly insisted.

"It's me, Abby, Dr. Kelly."

"Abby, what have you done?"

Maggie smiled brightly, seeing me.

"Nothing, I promise. It was Annie and Hutch. Annie pulled the plug on Maggie's machines and ran out."

"What? Why would she do that?" Maggie looked at me, confused.

"Abby, tell me exactly what you saw." Dr. Kelly was holding my shoulders, looking intensely at me.

"Annie and Hutch came in, and Annie said goodbye to Maggie. Hutch kept telling her they had to go, that Maggie wouldn't want them to get caught."

Dr. Kelly ran out of the room. I looked at Maggie,

happy to see her awake and alive.

"What's happening?" Maggie asked again.

One of the coats gave her a shot of something and she fell back.

"Abby don't let them ---" but she didn't finish her sentence before she was asleep again.

"What did you do?" I screamed.

"We need her to stay still. We have to make sure she's okay," one of the female Coats explained to me.

I was crying. I didn't understand what was happening.

"Is she going to be okay?"

"We will take care of her. You should go back to your Domicile."

Another Coat was quickly at my side to escort me

back to my Domicile. I looked back at Maggie. They were working feverishly around her.

The alarms silenced.

My escort hurried me out of the room and down the halls to my room. We didn't say a word as I stepped inside, and the door slid between us. I knew I wasn't going to be able to sleep, but I got into bed anyway. There was nothing I could do. I just had to wait and see what happened next. I'm not sure when, but I did finally fall asleep.

## Chapter 9

Growing up out in The Elements creates a certain type of person. Being taken from there, from everything I knew, and thrown into a life in the Estates was horribly traumatic. I cried myself to sleep every night until I met Maggie.

She was everything I wanted to be. I admired her strength and courage. I envied her relationship with her sister. I longed for a bond like they had. My brother Kyle left when we lost our parents, and I never saw him again. I hoped he was okay, wherever he ended up. Our Pride, The Bowery Pride, had three families in it. When Kyle left, they let me stay with them. They were nice to me, and I always felt a part of our Pride. Not like the story Maggie told me of what she and Annie went through after their parents died. Maggie was just a baby and didn't really remember. She only knew what Annie told her about them. From what Maggie had said, she didn't really remember much before she and Annie were out on their own. Uncle Joe and a little girl named Cassie were all she could recall from their Pride.

She said she wanted to join another Pride, but Annie never wanted to, so they were on their own for years before being brought to the Combine. I was thankful every day she was here. When I met her, I thought she was so strong and independent, and I wanted to be just like that. She was smart and athletic. She made it through our daily trials like it was nothing, while I struggled. I knew she was special, and I was happy she was my friend.

After "The Incident", as everyone in the Combine called it, all I visited was her shell. Wired up to so many machines. The first time I saw her, I cried. I missed her so much and wished there was something I could do to bring her back. Now, after seeing her awake, a new hope filled my heart and I had to figure out a way to keep her awake.

## Chapter 10

"Abby? Abby, are you okay?"

It was Cindy, my handler. She used to be Maggie's handler. I looked up at her. I hadn't been paying attention. All I could think about was Maggie. I hadn't gotten any news from anyone and was not allowed to visit her. I was worried and couldn't concentrate.

"Huh? Oh, yeah, I'm fine. What did you ask me?"

"Never mind. Tell me what's wrong. We can't continue if you're distracted."

"Have you not heard?"

"Heard what?"

 "Maggie, she woke up last night. Annie and Hutch

ran away. That's what the alarms were last night."

"What? No, I was at the wedding reception. How are we not on high alert?"

Cindy ran to the other Coats in the room and asked them. They didn't seem to know anything about it. I actually started questioning what I had seen.

"Abby, I think you may want to take the day off from trials today."

"Why?"

"Well, you're clearly distracted, so much so, you're making up stories, I'm not really sure why that's happening."

"I'm not --" I stopped myself, thinking better of it. If they were covering it up for some reason, not telling everyone, I didn't want to be the one to tell people and get in trouble.

"Okay," I conceded, "I'll take the day off."

"I think that's a good idea. I'll escort you back."

Walking past the other Coats, I could feel them watching me. They really didn't know.

I sat in my room, waiting for Cindy to make her way back to wherever it was she would go. Once I thought enough time had passed, I made my way to Maggie's room. I had long since memorized how to get there. I didn't really care if I got caught anymore. She was my only friend in The Combine, and I refused to lose her again.

Weaving through the hallways to Maggie's room, I was careful to not be seen. Not that it mattered, there were cameras everywhere. When I got there the room was dark. I opened the door to an empty space. All the machines were gone.

I ran back to my room and hit my call button.

"I need to speak to Dr. Kelly."

A voice from above answered me, "Dr. Kelly is not available."

"Someone had better find her for me, or I will tell everyone what I saw last night."

There was silence. I waited, staring into the camera in the corner of my Domicile.

"Abby, someone will be there shortly to escort you to my office."

"Unavailable, huh," I said out loud, to myself.

I waited again.

Tiny showed up to take me to Dr. Kelly. He looked tired.

We didn't say a word for the entirety of the walk. He had never escorted me before. He was usually reserved for the older Community members, or what I knew now to be the important ones, Annie, Maggie, and Kai.

I still couldn't believe everything that had happened with all of them. The story was never really clear. So many rumors spread quickly about Hutch killing Kai for attacking Annie and Maggie. Annie and Maggie in comas and Hutch being cast out. All of it too crazy not to be true.

Losing Maggie broke my heart. I still hoped every day I visited her she would wake up and I would have her back. I loved her so much and knew I couldn't bear losing her.

Dr. Kelly sat behind her desk. She also looked tired. Something major was happening.

"Hello, Abby." Her tone was angry. "First of all, we really don't appreciate threats. Second of all, you can be in a lot of trouble for sneaking out of your Domicile to visit Maggie like you have been. We have let it slide because we know how much you care about her. Our leniency is waning."

"Where's Maggie?" I figured I would get to the point instead of being scolded.

"Maggie is being taken care of; you don't have to worry about her."

"And Annie and Hutch? Where are they?"

"Annie and Hutch tried to escape and were terminated."

"Terminated? You killed them? Does Maggie know?" I was angry, not upset and I didn't really believe her. Annie was too smart to get caught. I was certain she and Hutch were safely far out in the barrens where The Staties would be too scared to go after them.

"Abby, I don't have time to argue with you or explain the laws of The Estates with you. Your purpose here is to help further the Savior Project. You should go back to your trials and forget about everything you have seen, heard or think you know before your usefulness runs out."

I had gotten much stronger since they brought me to the Combine, more confident and mature. I didn't have anyone since Maggie went into her coma. I could only depend on myself. Dr. Kelly's threat to cast me out did scare me but I wasn't about to let her know that.

"Now, go. I don't want to hear from you again."

I rose to leave then leaned into Dr. Kelly my hands on her desk in front of her, "I'm not afraid of you or of being cast out. I just want to see Maggie. I don't care about anything else. I don't have anything else. I'm all alone here. Maggie was my only friend. I know you don't care about how we live here if we are happy, or not. All the Community members you have brought here do the best they can to find relationships and happiness. They have people their age they can talk to and be with. Maggie was mine and she was taken away. So, now I have no one. If there is a chance, I can have her back, I need to know. I will continue being your test subject, just let me see her."

"Maggie is undergoing a very important and very dangerous operation right now."

"What kind of operation?"

Dr. Kelly sighed conceding.

"We have to extract the 2nd Gen she is carrying. Turning off the machines caused many complications."

"Is she going to be okay?"

114

"We think she will. We don't know about the baby."

"Maggie's baby might die?"

"The 2nd Gen is not Maggie's, Abby, she was too young to extract an egg to fertilize. We implanted her with a fertilized embryo from Anne and Malakai."

"Will the baby die?"

"We don't know. We are trying to prevent that from happening, which is why you can't see her."

We stood there staring at each other for a long moment. I wasn't satisfied and she wasn't budging.

"Look, Abby, I understand how important Maggie is to you. She is especially important to us too. As is the Second Gen she is carrying. When we are certain everyone is safe, I will make sure you get to see her."

"So, you won't put her back into a coma?"

"No, if she stays awake and the operation is a success. We will not induce another coma. The fact that she woke up on her own after the machines were turned off, is quite an extraordinary development."

"She's special, right?"

"You all are Abby. All First Gens are special. Not all of you have shown the same development. You all have evolved in some way though."

"I'm not special like them, am I."

"Not like Anne and Maggie, no. It doesn't mean you're any less important to the Savior Project. Now, please, be patient. I promise to let you know Maggie's status."

"Why haven't you told any of the other Coats what has happened?"

"We don't want to create a panic. As far as they all know, we found an answer to preserving our future in Hutch and Anne. If they know, they may react badly. We want to avoid that, so it is particularly important you keep all of this to yourself."

"I understand."

"Good, now please, I have much work to do." She said it waving her hand dismissing me and looked down at the tablet she held in front of her.

"Thank you, Dr. Kelly."

She didn't look up and I left her office. Tiny was waiting for me outside her door to take me back to my Domicile. We walked in silence most of the way. Turn after turn through the familiar hallways, I was afraid to look at him when I said it.

"Tiny, they're not dead are they."

The big man didn't say anything. When we got to my Domicile, he waited a beat before my door slid shut on him and winked at me.

## Chapter 11

### *LUTHER "TINY" TYSON*

When the loud high alert alarm sounded, and I immediately knew my mistake. I should have known Annie would do this. I knew she wouldn't just allow them to keep testing her sister. I cursed myself for giving them an escape route right past Maggie's room. I should have known.

It was all so crazy. Everything they had done to these poor kids. They didn't ask for any of it. And I was part of it all. Still standing outside Abby's Domicile I leaned against a wall exhausted from the last twenty-four hours. I recalled the last year in the Combine. It was a year of discovery and development. More so than ever before. They had been studying The Elements for years already. Setting up cameras to watch how The Commons coped with the harsh conditions.  Dr. Sanford's studies of the First Gen Colonists proved the presence of the evolutionary changes. He knew The First Gen Commons would have evolved as well and needed to see just how much.

We had brought in some who weren't First Gens, we needed a baseline to compare to.  I signed on right away unhappy with their plans. I wanted to keep an eye on what they were doing.  I tried to help some of them escape only to discover they liked being there. They liked being inside safe from The Elements.

When they brought the sisters in, I thought they would be like all the rest.  But they found what they were looking for in them. And Malakai, he was special too.  The difference was palpable. You could feel the excitement of the scientists. They were buzzing.

I suspected their intentions with Hutch.  He was

assigned to the sisters long before they were brought in because his father and Dr. Sanford needed a First Gen Commonist, as they coined it, from him.  They planted the seeds early and it was successful. Hutch was in love with Anne well before the sisters were brought in. I didn't know what lengths they were willing to go.

Poor Malakai. He was a good kid. They started with him almost immediately. His meals and the shake he was given were loaded with extra hormones.  They even started injecting him with human growth hormones and steroids. I tried to talk to him, tell him what they were doing there. He was like the others, he wanted to be there despite everything.  I could tell when he started skipping breakfast it was getting worse. But I was too late. I didn't see him on the day of "The Incident" as they called it.

Dr. Sanford was getting impatient. They needed a

Second Gen and he was prepared to do whatever was necessary. He intercepted Malakai who was coming to see me to arrange another visit to Annie's Domicile. Dr. Sanford knew he was running out of time. They needed it for their research. So, he injected Malakai with even more of what they were already giving him and let him in to see Annie.

If Dr. Sanford had waited, he would have seen Anne and Hutch's growing relationship. His impatience cost Malakai his life almost killed both Anne and Maggie and made Hutch a killer.

It was such a mess. I knew long before all of it I needed to get those kids out. Annie was the first to seem to not want to be there. She was suspicious of everything. Rebelling every chance she got. Maggie was happy. She was happy to be warm and fed. She was building a life for herself there.

I watched them closely. All of them. I wanted to

122

warn them to tell them what was planned for them. I don't know why I didn't. Instead, I listened and waited. I should never have waited. Now it was too late. So much had gone wrong.

Sitting in the dark in my Domicile I contemplated my next move. So far, no one had suspected me of anything. I had responded to the alarms as I normally would have and nobody asked me any questions but I knew it wouldn't be long before Dr. Kelly called for me to ask what part I had in all of it. I wasn't sure what I would say if asked directly.

Just as I was about to turn some lights on a voice from above ordered me to Dr. Kelly's office. This was it. It was time to face whatever it was she would have for me. I didn't really care. I did right by those kids. I knew Dr. Kelly and Dr. Sanford wouldn't agree. The future of The Estates and everyone in them depended on the research on the baby Annie was carrying. I was hoping the other one, the one they would extract from Maggie would be enough and they wouldn't search for Hutch and Annie. I would find out when I got Dr. Kelly's office.

## Chapter 12

"Tiny, please sit down." Dr. Kelly's voice was terse and annoyed. I sat down across from her my hands on my lap. She looked at me over the black-rimmed glasses she wore at the end of her nose.

"We haven't had the chance to talk about the events of the past two days. With everything that was happening with Maggie we didn't have the opportunity to figure out exactly what happened with Anne and Hutch."

I tried to appear nonplussed. I shifted slightly in the metal folding chair I sat in. It was uncomfortable for a person my size. It creaked under my weight.

"Only a few members of The Savior Project know they have escaped. Myself, Dr. Sanford, the guards

125

who chased after them, and you."

"Were they recovered?"

"No!" Dr. Kelly screamed, slamming her hands down on the metal desk in front of her as she stood up. Her face was red with anger.

I flinched and leaned back away from her. I had never seen her lose her cool before. She was always so even-tempered and in control.

"They're gone. They disappeared. They searched for as long as they could take the cold which wasn't very long, and they've checked the footage of the cameras in the area. Nothing. We know you know something. You need to tell me where they are."

"Dr. Kelly, I am very sorry, I do not know where they are." It wasn't a lie. I didn't know. According to the plan they were to head straight for Annie's old campsite to pick up supplies then they would head

126

further out into the barrens to set up a new camp to wait and have the baby. I was slated to meet with them in a few weeks when everything had quieted down.

"I know you know something, Luther Tyson. I have no idea why you would help them, but I do know, you are no longer welcome on The Savior Project. I want you to pack your things and leave this Estate."

"Dr. Kelly, you just used my full name for the first time since I've known you and you're telling me, Luther Tyson, that I need to leave the Tyson Estate?"

Now it was Dr. Kelly's turn to shift. In her blind fury, it seemed she forgot I was the direct heir to Calvin Tyson and The Estate would be under my control in the coming years.

We stood staring at each other for a moment before she finally spoke again, much more calmly this time.

127

"Okay, I'm sorry. It is a very tense time right now. So much was riding on successfully implanting those Commons."

"You really only see them as subjects. You know they're real people, just like me and you."

"They're a means to an end. A solution to our very big problem."

"Wow."

"Look. maybe I am a horrible person, but I am a horrible person who is trying to save us."

"Right, I guess if you keep telling yourself that, you can clear your conscience."

"My conscience is clear. How about yours, Tiny? Is there anything you would like to tell me about how Hutch and Anne escaped?"

"No, I can honestly say there is not."

## Chapter 13

Well, I didn't lie.

After leaving Dr. Kelly frustrated and angry, I made my way to where they had moved Maggie. I knew the extraction was successful and she was recovering. I wanted to see what, if anything, she remembered from that night and most importantly to see if she was alright.

The hallways were empty, everyone was at their various assigned spots in trials. It was quiet and peaceful, unlike it had been the past twenty-four hours.

Despite my attempts not to, I had grown to care for these kids. Daryl warned me not to get too close. He knew me better than anyone. Though we were only cousins we were raised like brothers. Twins really, only three weeks apart. My mother died in childbirth. I almost died too being horribly premature. Everyone said I was the smallest baby they'd ever seen survive. That's why everyone started calling me Tiny.

Daryl's father, Dwayne Tyson, was my father's baby brother and was far down the line to inherit control of The Tyson Estate. He and his family left to live in The Bloch Estate when he became the pastor there. It was natural for Daryl to follow in his footsteps.

My father, Calvin Tyson IV, was the oldest of four boys. He inherited The Estate when my grandfather finally passed away at a hundred and eight years old. He was the oldest surviving Estate Head when he died. Old Lady Faulkner lived to be a hundred and ten breaking his record four years later.

My father started running The Tyson Estate alongside his father as Calvin Tyson III advanced in years and still ran it now at eighty-seven. I have not been groomed to take it over. The Estate Heads had a Board of Directors helping them run things now. It had basically turned into just a title more than a power position. No real grooming was necessary. If the Board didn't find the next heir fit, they would choose from the immediate family. I was the last in the immediate line of the Tyson's and it would end with me as I never married and would likely not ever produce an heir.

In our Estate, no one fought for the position. Other Estates weren't as lucky. Siblings constantly fighting over who was in power. Sometimes taking things too far. The worst I had heard happened in the Crane Estate where brothers actually fought to the death to take claim of the open seat.

I was free to do whatever I wanted and then I could take the helm of The Estate or not. If I didn't want it, the Board would choose someone else from my family. If they carried the Tyson name, it was really the only prerequisite they cared about.

I chose to join The Savior Project to oversee what their plans were. I am not a scientist. I don't understand all the mumbo jumbo they do. I do understand the difference between right and wrong. What they were doing was wrong.

Growing up, Daryl and I learned all about our very important great, great, grandfather, who all in our family simply called grandfather. It was hard growing up with his legacy on our shoulders. Though much of it was just history now and so much had changed. The number of Estates grew from the four originals, Tyson, Faulkner, Wilkes, and Bloch to the eight that stood now with the Winchester, Crane, Gilmore and

Taxter Estates.  The Tyson Estate was one of the smallest now.

When I joined The Savior Project it was still in its infancy.  They were just starting to figure out what to study and how to study it.  Sending people outside to retrieve samples of the earth outside the bubbles. Then setting up cameras to observe the Commons. When they brought the first batch of recruits in, they weren't chosen for any particular reason, they were just the easiest ones to catch.

At first, the Commons fought for their freedom. Proving to be difficult to test. Dr. Sanford and his team learned how to accommodate them in a way that would make them want to stay.  And it worked. Commons were happy to be there after the initial shock of being taken by force wore off. I watched as they fell into their routines and grew comfortable with their surroundings.

I was there to help corral people and keep them in line with my intimidating stature. I never spoke to anyone because I was told by the doctors, it made me more intimidating. People tended to forget who my father was, and I was fine with that. I went along with everything, even the trackers if I didn't have to get one.

I met Hutch when he was just a boy. When his mother died, I went to the funeral. I was there when his father gave him the picture of Anne and told him he would be part of The Savior Project. I watched him study the girls and learn as much as he could about them. I watched him design Annie and Maggie's Domicile. I watched him take over as Annie's Handler. And I watched him fall in love with her. Then I had to watch what happened to him after "The Incident".

I was the one who brought him out when he was

expelled.  He begged me to not leave him there and it took every bit of self-control I had not to bring him back with me.  From safe inside our Estate security paddock, I watched him get beat up and his food stolen. I watched him get sick when he was forced to eat from the garbage.  I watched him cry himself to sleep.  It broke my heart to do nothing.

Inside, I watched as they did the unthinkable to the sisters.  Inducing comas and implanting them with their experimental embryos.  I watched them in their forced slumber, their bellies growing with the hope of the Estates within them and could do nothing.

I watched and did nothing.

It was all by design.  It hadn't taken them very long to figure out what they were looking for and to decide what they needed to do to get it and they got it.

At least Hutch and Annie were out now.  I wondered

where they ended up. I hoped they were alright. I would have to be careful about asking questions or accessing any of the video footage to see where they went. I wouldn't want to spark any suspicion.

I found Maggie asleep. She was still hooked up to be monitored. Her swollen belly was gone. The fact these people ever thought implanting a ten-year-old with an embryo was okay, shows just how morally bankrupt they truly are.

All they cared about was finding their solution.

All I cared about was getting as many of the Commons out before they could be disposed of.

The big secret.

When a Common's usefulness ended, if they didn't show the evolution the scientists sought, they were euthanized and incinerated. Never to be thought of again. They weren't cast out; they were disposed of. I had only witnessed one. They injected them with something that made them go to sleep then they never woke up. It was disgusting. How little they cared for human life if they were saving themselves, the means justified the end, at least in their eyes.

It was after I saw my first "disposal" that I went to Daryl with a tracker to see if he could help figure out how to deactivate it. I knew he had smart people he trusted in The Bloch Estate with him. It took a long time before they came up with the tech to do it. Once they did, I started to try and help the Commons who were brought in. Until Annie showed up, none of the Commons showed any interest in going back out into The Elements.

Dr. Kelly was brought in to help with the girls. Dr. Sanford thought they would respond better to a woman. Dr. Kelly was a force. She was incredibly intelligent. Smarter than both Dr. Sanford and Dr.

Alexander combined.  They knew it too. At first, I think they felt threatened. Then I think it grew into respect and relief that they had her on their team. She advanced their research leaps and bounds when she got there using technology the men hadn't thought of to test different parts of the evolutionary effects of The Shift.

Everything happened much faster when she arrived which made Daryl and I work faster to find a solution.  It was all I could do to not tell the Malakai, Annie, Maggie, and Hutch what was planned for them. I was afraid if I did, they would try to escape without a plan and get themselves killed.

Anne proved to be the most evolved.  I knew they would want the most from her as soon as I saw her x-ray.  She was special. She held the key to The Savior Project. I knew it would be even harder to help them.

Lost in my thoughts and memories, I didn't notice

138

Abby standing next to me in the doorway to the operatory Maggie was in.

"How is she doing?"

"She looks stable but I'm no doctor. I can trust you, right, Abby?"

"Of course, I just want to make sure Maggie is alright."

Abby went to Maggie's bedside and held her hand. I knew she wasn't in a coma anymore. They did have her heavily sedated. I left knowing I wouldn't be able to get any information from her yet. It would have to wait until she was awake. Now I had to inconspicuously access some video and try to find Anne and Hutch.

## Chapter 14

It was late. I knew Parker Stone would be manning the security paddock, he was one of the few people who knew about Hutch and Annie escaping. We were friendly. I didn't know much about him other than he took great pleasure from his role in security. Sometimes too much. He probably wouldn't be the best person to help me, but I couldn't wait any longer. I needed to know if Anne and Hutch were alright. Knowing Anne, they would find a way to survive. She knew how to do that better than anything. Still, I was worried about them.

We were scheduled to reconnect, and I had no idea where they were. In all actuality, it was a good thing, if I didn't know where they were Dr. Kelly and Dr. Sanford definitely didn't know.

"Hey, Parker."

"Hey, Tiny. What are you doing down here?"

"Checking to see if you've seen anything on our two escapees."

"Yeah, but it's like they just disappeared, poof!" The older man flicked his hands in the air like he was completing a magic trick. "Here look."

He punched something into the keyboard in front of him and three of the monitors switched to a new image.

Was he volunteering me the information? That was unexpected and fruitful.

"See, here they are leaving the complex out of the Southwest Corridor. They run about here." He froze the video.

142

I could see them running holding hands.

Pointing to another monitor, "you can see them here too."

Then to the last screen, "and here too."

I could see them clearly.

"Then she lets his hand go. They run a bit more and he disappears."

He was right. Hutch was there one second then the next he was gone. Poof.

"Then she goes to where he was, looks around, stops and then she disappears."

He rewound it a couple of times to show me again.

"See, poof!"

"Yeah, I see. That's crazy."

"Tell me about it.  It took me a long time to find this footage too.  But I found it!"

"Yeah, great work.  I'm sure Dr. Kelly is pleased."

"Oh, I just found it.  She doesn't know about it yet."

"Oh wow, you just found this?  Do you want me to bring it to Dr. Kelly?"

"Would you do that for me?  It would be a huge help. I'd rather not trek all the way to her office with it. The file is too big to send. Here, it's all on this."

He handed me a small plastic square.

"She just has to plug it into her tablet.  She knows how to do it. Thanks, man."

"Sure, no problem."

I wasn't really sure what to make of everything.  I thought for sure they would be on high alert to not

144

let me near any of the security footage and now it was being handed to me. Was it serendipitous or was I being set up?

He turned back to his monitors and the feed we watched, returned to the live feeds.

Video in hand I left Parker. Back in the hall, I had a decision to make. Did I bring the video to Dr. Kelly or wait and go out to see if I could find them myself first?

I had only been out in The Elements twice and didn't welcome the idea of heading out there again, especially without knowing where I was going. At least with this information, I had an idea where they were last.

If I gave Dr. Kelly the video, she would send people out there to look for them. I could volunteer to head the search party. I headed towards Dr. Kelly's Office.

If I didn't give her the video, it would give me time to figure out what to do and find them. I headed back to my Domicile.

If I didn't give her the video and she found out, it would be bad. I headed toward Dr. Kelly's office.

If I waited and watched it a couple more times myself, I could try to figure out what went wrong and where they went. I headed back to my Domicile.

If I was being set up, then giving her the video would be unexpected. I headed back toward Dr. Kelly's office.

"Tiny, are you alright?" It was Parker.

"Yeah, why?"

"I thought you were going to bring that to Dr. Kelly."

"I am." I had to think quickly. I probably looked

ridiculous walking back and forth changing directions. "I have to go to the bathroom, so I was deciding whether or not to take care of that first or go straight to her office."

"Why don't you just use the hall bathroom right there?"

"Because it's the kind of bathroom trip you want to take in your own space if you get my meaning."

He laughed. I joined him in his laughter for a moment then left in the direction of Dr. Kelly's office.

## Chapter 15

"Tiny, I wasn't expecting to see you tonight. It's late. What can I help you with?" Dr. Kelly sat at her desk. She looked tired and stressed. Her hair was down, and her lab coat hung on the back of her chair. Things were clearly not going well.

"Actually, I think I can help you. This is from Parker Stone."

I placed the small plastic square onto her desk.

"What is it?"

I watched her closely. I couldn't tell if she knew about it or not.

"It's the video footage of the Commons escaping."

"He found something." She picked it up quickly and plugged it into her tablet. If she did know about it, she was doing an extraordinary job hiding it.

The image projected above her tablet. I pointed out what Parker had pointed out to me.

"Why did Parker give this to you?"

"He didn't want to walk all the way here from his post."

It wasn't a lie. If I didn't have to tell her I went there to check out the feed, I certainly wasn't going to offer up that information.

She studied the footage, rewinding and pausing, zooming in on parts. I stayed silent. She looked up at me as if she had forgotten I was standing there.

"You can go."

I turned to leave but stopped.

"Dr. Kelly, would you like me to put a search team together?"

She looked up at me, her eyes suspicious.

"I don't know if that's a good idea."

"Okay, well, let me know if you change your mind. Goodnight, Dr. Kelly."

On my way back to my Domicile I stopped to see Maggie. She was awake.

"Tiny!" She shouted upon seeing me.

"Hello, Margaret."

"Oh my God, you talk?"

"Yes, I have a voice. How are you feeling?" I couldn't help but smile at her.

"Like I've been asleep for a few years."

Her color was bright. She looked healthy and strong despite being hooked up to what looked like a hundred monitors.

"Tiny, no one will tell me anything and I know, I can't get up. I tried and I tore my stitches. I was bleeding all over the place then passed out again. I just woke up a little bit ago and no one has answered my calls."

"How much do you know, Maggie."

"Nothing. I don't even know why I have these stitches."

Well, I wasn't about to be the one to drop the bomb on her.

"Can you fill in some blanks for me?"

"I can't, Maggie. We need to let Dr. Kelly bring you up

to speed. I will call for her and let her know you are awake."

"Like she doesn't already know."

"You're quite right Maggie, I do know." Dr. Kelly breezed past me to Maggie's bedside.

I was curious about how she would break the news to her about everything that had gone on while she was in her coma.

"Tiny, you can go."

"No, I want him to stay."

"Maggie, I need to speak to you in private."

"Anything you have to say to me, Tiny can hear."

"It's alright Maggie, I'll come back." I started to leave.

"No, I want you here, Tiny. It's obvious something has happened to Annie or she would be here and stalling."

Dr. Kelly started to tell Maggie the very long story that brought us to this point.

I watched as Maggie processed everything Dr. Kelly said. How Malakai attacked her and Annie. That Malakai was dead. How Hutch was expelled for killing him. How she and Annie were in comas and implanted with embryos. How Hutch and Annie got married. Then about the baby, she had carried for six months who was now in an isolet being cared for by strangers.

Her face was expressionless. There was too much. I could see it. I think I saw the exact moment it happened. Maggie made a decision in those moments of Dr. Kelly's recap of events. I wasn't sure what that decision was, but it was clear something profound had changed in her.

She didn't speak right away. We all sat in a bubble of silence floating for what seemed like forever.

"Dr. Kelly. Where is my sister now?" Her voice was even, calm.

"We don't know Maggie. We may have pinpointed where she and Hutch disappeared. But we don't have more information than that."

"I don't want you to look for them."

"What?"

"I want you to leave them alone."

I was as shocked as Dr. Kelly.

"If what you're telling me is true, you have everything you need with me. You have a Second Gen Common. I think that's probably more valuable than a, what did

154

you call it?  A Commonist?  If me, Annie and Kai evolved the way you say we have, the fact that the child I carried is theirs and grew as a part of me, pretty much makes him the most important person in this world right now.  So, leave my sister and Hutch alone and do whatever you need to do with me and the child you created."

She sounded strong and wise well beyond her eleven years.

"Maggie, we have to look for them and make sure they're alright."

"They're fine, I know it.  If something had happened to Annie, I would feel it."

I didn't know what Dr. Kelly would do.  I had hoped when we were making our plan for their escape, Dr. Kelly and the rest of them would let Anne and Hutch go knowing they still had Maggie and the child she carried.

"I can't believe you thought any of this was okay. I can tell you, it's not okay, not at all." Maggie looked away from us then. Her head hanging in defeat.

"Alright, Maggie. I need you to get some sleep. You still have a lot of healing to do."

I wasn't sure what to make of what was going on. I didn't think Maggie was going to appreciate being given orders by Dr. Kelly again. She had a lot of Annie in her.

"Where's Abby? I want to see Abby."

"Alright Maggie, Tiny, will you go get Abby?"

"Of course, Dr. Kelly." I turned to leave.

"Tiny, do you know where they are?" Maggie sounded hopeful.

"I'm sorry, Maggie, I don't."

Dr. Kelly looked at me. She didn't believe I knew nothing about their escape. She wasn't wrong.

"I will go get Abby; she is going to be very excited to see you awake."

She smiled at me and I left to get Abby.

## Chapter 16

A few days had passed, and I was never asked to put a search party together. I had no idea if Hutch and Annie were even alive.

My schedule was a mess. I didn't have any normalcy since that night. I constantly felt on edge not knowing when someone would figure out my role in their escape. They obviously knew I was involved. No one had figured out the access key they used was mine. Or if they had, there was no mention of it to me.

I felt lost, wandering the halls, escorting random Commons to lunch and dinner. I had no focus. I had spent the last year with an assignment and now it was gone.

Sitting in my Domicile I started to feel claustrophobic. I made the decision I needed to look for them. Find out if they were alright. I would speak to Dr. Kelly and *tell* her I was putting a search party together instead of suggesting it.

I went to breakfast where I saw Maggie and Abby. It was nice to see Maggie out of bed. She looked healthy. She and Abby looked very happy eating together. They seemed oblivious to all the stares from the Coats who had no idea what had happened and were confused to see Maggie. I didn't want to disturb them, but Maggie called me over to join them. I never would have sat with them before. Now, it seemed like the natural thing to do. We all shared a story. A story that still needed a conclusion. We didn't know where it was going. We did know, though unspoken to each other, it was a journey we were taking together.

"Hey, Tiny," Abby looked up with a smile.

"Good morning, girls."

"Tiny, can you tell me anything about what happened?"

"I don't know much, Margaret."

"Okay, I get it, can't talk here. I'll try again another time."

I smirked. She was smart like her sister.

We sat and enjoyed breakfast. The last time I enjoyed a meal was at Hutch and Annie's wedding. It seemed so long ago when it had only been a couple of weeks. When we finished breakfast, I offered to escort them wherever they needed to go next.

Leaving the Dining Hall, I could hear whispers follow us out. Everyone was on edge. The rumors had started with people only having bits and pieces of the real stories some very tall tales were born.

After "The Incident" everything changed. Most had never experienced anything like it. A Colonist killing a Common. It was a big deal. Hutch being expelled scared a lot of the Coats. We lost a lot of members of The Savior Project. Many moved out of The Tyson Estate. In the three months Anne was in her coma, a dark cloud hovered over the project and everyone involved in it.

The wedding had been the exact distraction we all needed. People were happy again and things seemed to normalize.

Now, after word of the escape trickled out, despite Dr. Kelly and Dr. Sanford's attempts to keep it a secret, people were dropping out of the project and moving away from The Tyson Estate again.

My father asked to see me to find out what was happening. I didn't tell him much he didn't already know. The only person who knew my involvement in the escape was Daryl. I trusted he wouldn't say anything.

News of the escape slowly permeated the other Estates as well. I received a note from Ella Luciana, the designer of Anne's wedding dress, asking me what happened. Daryl had even sent a note. I assumed to throw off any suspicions of his involvement. I knew if he was asked a direct question he would not lie. I hoped it wouldn't come to that. There didn't seem to be much investigation into what happened at all which I thought was odd and out of character for everyone involved.

I wandered the Trials area and the operatories to see if anyone needed anything before heading back to my room.

Returning to my Domicile, I found another note. It was not on stationery from any other Estate. I opened it curious.

> *Anne and Hutch are alive. They are*
> *safe for the time being. Please tell*
> *Maggie. Please do not look for*
> *them, their safety depends on it.*
>
> ~    *A Friend*

I studied the note. There were no identifying marks or any signs of where it came from. The handwriting was not familiar. I looked around my Domicile. It had to have been left while I was at breakfast. I immediately headed to the security paddock to see if the cameras had captured anything.

Parker was there again.

"Hey, Tiny, you look stressed, what's going on."

"Parker, can you pull up the footage from E Corridor for the last hour for me please?"

"Sure, why, what's up?"

I didn't have time for his questions. I tried to calm my impatience.

"Someone dropped something off at my Domicile and I want to see who left it."

"It was probably one of the messenger kids or something. No big deal."

"Yeah, probably, I just want to know who so I can ask them a question."

"Okay, here." His plump rosy hands punch his keyboard and the screen in front of came to life. "Wait a minute."

The screen went blank.

The timestamp read 07:18 AM then jumped to 08:23 AM.

"What the hell?" Parker fiddled with the keys in front of him again tapping away.

"There's no footage?"

"I don't understand. It looks like we went dark from 7:18 AM until 8:23 AM. Like an hour and five-minute glitch."

"What? Is that normal?"

"Not even a little."

"What do you have?"

"Well, let's see. We have you leaving your Domicile at 6:52 AM. We have a couple of others exiting and walking through, I'm assuming to the Dining Hall for breakfast."

He fast-forwarded a bit.

"Then, see here, we go dark at 7:18 AM and it jumps to 8:23 AM then there's nothing until you return to your Domicile at 8:32 AM."

"Why would this happen?"

"I honestly don't know.  We have hiccups time and again as you would with any closed-circuit surveillance equipment.  It just seems crazy it would happen right when you needed to see it."

"Yes, it certainly does."

"Sorry, man, there's no way to recover something that isn't there."

Is there any way to tell who may have had access to shut it down?"

I had done it myself for Kai and Maggie and so far, no

one had traced it back to me.  It was possible they didn't have a way to tell who had accessed the CCTV.

"No, *I* don't but maybe Dr. Sanford or Dr. Kelly can."

I thought about it for a moment.  Did I really want to get them involved?  Probably not.

"Don't worry about it, Parker.  I'll go ask the messenger kids.  I'm sure I'll figure it out."

Parker shrugged and went back to securing or whatever it was he did all day.  I made my way back to my Domicile to study the note to see if there was anything that could identify who it came from.

I was happy to know the kids were alright assuming the letter was true.  It left so many questions. Now, I knew I had to do something.

Who could this friend be?

## Chapter 17

### *ANNE ALEXANDER*

It was time. The baby was coming. I didn't know how I knew but I knew. The day before I had spent cleaning and preparing the baby's room. Hutch called it "nesting". He knew so much more about what I was going through than I did.

The weeks that had passed since The Exordium were relatively uneventful. Hutch and I kept to ourselves. People surprisingly left us alone. We were very conscious of what we talked about in the living room and bedroom. We were used to it from our time together in mine and Maggie's Domicile in the Combine.

We reserved any talk about leaving for the baby's

room.  There really wasn't much of it. We knew we weren't going anywhere until after Eden was born. We were living a fairly normal existence. Aside from attending service every other day to keep up appearances to Jessup and the rest of the flock. Everyone was nice. Hutch and I even went to dinner at other family's Dwellings occasionally. We spent time with Uncle Joe, mostly him visiting us since Magda didn't like me.  We ate with Jacob's family the most. Mary Elizabeth and I became friends. I asked her a lot of questions about having a baby. She didn't like the questions at first but warmed up to me.  I think she felt bad for me. I welcomed the information. I was terrified about what I was about to go through.

We were assigned a doula.  We had doulas out in The Elements.  They helped the women of The Community have their babies.  I had never witnessed a birth. I was taken away when Maggie was born.  I

did hear the screams of women giving birth. It was
why I was so scared. Thinking about the pain that
would provoke that kind of scream was horrifying.

"Hutch, I think it's time."

Hutch leaped out of our bed. He started running
around in circles. I giggled watching him.

"Clothes, I need clothes. Do you need clothes?"

"We need to call for the doula." I tried to get out of
bed when a white-hot pain shot through my back and
down both of my legs. I cried out. Hutch was
immediately by my side. I felt beads of sweat form on
my forehead.

"What can I do?" Hutch looked almost in tears.

I shook my head. The pain passed and I was able to
speak again, "get our doula. She'll know what to do."

"Will you be alright if I leave you?"

"Yes, go." I was wrong. As soon as he left another wave of pain gripped me hard. I grabbed the blankets covering me gathering them in my hands and squeezed tight, my knuckles white, my teeth clenched. I was crying now. The pain was unbelievable.

As quickly as it came, it subsided again. I cursed myself for letting Hutch leave me. I looked around for something, anything that could help me. Anticipating the pain to return, I was surprised when someone knocked on the door.

"Anne, it's Mary Elizabeth, I saw Hutch. He asked me to come to you."

"Oh yes, please, come in." I could feel relief wash over me. She would know what to do until the doula got here.

Mary Elizabeth made her way into our bedroom to find me crying on our bed. She rushed to my side. I grabbed her hand. I was so happy to see her.

"Okay, it's going to be okay. Women do this every day. Just hold on to my hand and breathe through the pain."

"I had no idea it was going to hurt this much."

"Yes, and it's not going to get easier. You have to steady your breathing."

I tried to do as she said. I could feel the next wave of pain coming. She breathed in a pattern to show me.

She exhaled, quick, quick, slow. I mimicked her, Quick, quick, slow.

"Good, good job, Anne."

I continued to breathe like that until the pain passed

again. I felt light-headed. I held Mary Elizabeth's hand waiting for more pain. I was drenched with sweat and desperately wanted Hutch back. I couldn't fathom my mother going through this twice, or anyone for that matter. It was the worst pain I'd ever experienced, and I knew it was only going to get worse.

Mary Elizabeth continued to whisper soothing words to me as wave after wave of pain came more frequently and closer together. After what felt like a lifetime Hutch showed up with Sarah, our doula. She came in and swiftly changed me out of my wet nightgown and put fresh dry sheets on the bed. I let her take care of me. She propped me up on a dozen pillows and told Hutch and Mary Elizabeth to get hot water and clean towels. They did as they were told and Sarah told me to relax, everything would be fine.

I couldn't imagine anything ever being fine after this.

I couldn't stop crying. I felt like I was dying. My head was pounding, my heart was racing. I was so scared. Sarah kept telling me I needed to calm down. I couldn't steady myself.

"I don't feel well."

"It's completely normal, just relax and..."

Sarah's voice trailed off as I lost focus on her. The room spun. I looked at Hutch, His face was twisted with fear. I tried to speak. No words came and everything went black.

## Chapter 18

It was cold.  A cold I remembered well.  I felt piles of clothes on me.  I could see the fog of my breath.  A crackling fire snapped drawing my attention.  It was a strong fire. The warmth of it growing as I approached it.

"Annie?" a small voice I knew very well came from behind me.

I turned expecting to see Maggie.  No one was there.  Sadness overcame me as I stared at the empty bed my sister once slept in.

"Anne?" a boy's voice I knew very well came from behind me.

I spun around expecting to see Malakai.  No one was

there. I didn't understand why I was back in our campsite. I looked down to see my flat stomach. It had been so long since I'd seen it that way. I placed my hand there to confirm it. It was indeed empty.

The smell of burning wood suddenly became overwhelming. I started to cough. I stepped away from the fire its heat unbearable.

Stumbling backward I fell into my chair. The tattered stuffed chair Maggie and I dragged from our old campsite. Looking down I saw the lace of my boot. I remembered I had planned to mend it before it gave out completely. It was mended. I didn't remember fixing it.

In the corner sat Uncle Joe's baseball bat. It was shiny, brand new.

"Annie!" I heard Uncle Joe's voice. "Annie, look out!"

I turned to see Jessup. He had the baseball bat held high in the air above me about to strike.

I rolled out the way. A loud thud of metal hitting cushion sounded and a cloud of dust sprouted from the chair. I got up on the ready to defend myself. Jessup was gone.

I shook my head closing my eyes. Confusion and fear creeping in. The ground crunched under my boots. The fire died down to smoldering embers. I needed to tend to it. I made my way around our camp to find more things to burn. I picked up papers and books. As I threw them on the fire, I realized the books were bibles from the Sub Terra church. I looked down at my gloved hands. The wooden cross I wore for The Exordium sat in the palm of my hand. I stared at it for a long moment. It started to heat up and then suddenly burst into flames. I dropped it into the fire pulling my hand back to blow on the singed yarn of my glove.

I sat back down.  This time onto the couch in my Domicile.  The piles of clothes I wore replaced with Combine whites.  My eyes darted around. I caught sight of Uncle Joe's baseball bat again sitting in the corner.  Just like before, it was bright and shined like new.

I walked to it, picking it up.  The metal cool in my hands. I gripped it the way Uncle Joe had taught me. I swung it freely in front of me. It slammed hard into something. I glanced up in time to see a look of horror on Dr. Kelly's face as the bat connected with her sending her sailing across the room.  I felt the sting of a needle in the side of my neck. I dropped the bat my hands finding my throat. I looked up to see Tiny.

"I'm not going to let anything happen to you, Anne. Now, wake up!"

I woke to a white ceiling. The artificial light I had grown accustomed to in Sub Terra, blanketed my space. I was not in my Dwelling. I didn't know where I was.

"Hutch?" I sat up. My belly was small. Eden. Where was my baby? Was this real or was I still dreaming? I looked around; the room was empty. No furnishings at all save the bed I was lying in. I started to panic.

"Hutch!" I screamed, fear bubbling up quickly.

I didn't feel any pain. I couldn't understand what was happening. Where was I? Where was Eden? Was she alright? Just as I was about to get out of bed Hutch walked in the room carrying something very small wrapped in a pink blanket.

He smiled broadly as he handed me the bundle.

He kissed my forehead and whispered, "Anne, meet Eden."

180

## Chapter 19

"How can I love someone so much who I just met?" My heart was full. Tears were in my eyes. She was the most beautiful thing I had ever seen. She was perfect in every way. A pink knitted hat covered her tiny head. Her eyes opened and closed, and she yawned. She had the softest tuft of dark hair. I couldn't fathom the fact she was in my belly all that time and now I was holding her in my arms.

"I know, it's pretty incredible. So are you." Hutch kissed me softly then rubbed noses with Eden.

I tried to sit up and Hutch gently put a hand on my shoulder to stop me.

"Anne, you and the baby were in distress. They had to sedate you and operate to get Eden out."

"Operate? Who did that? Where are we?"

"This is Sub Terra's hospital. We had to rush you here when you lost consciousness. "

"I don't feel any pain."

"They gave you something for that. It's important you rest and heal." It was Sarah, my doula, walking through the door to join us.

"I didn't even know there was a hospital down here, much less a doctor."

"We aren't completely primitive down here." It was Jessup.

I shifted not expecting to see him. I didn't like that he was there. I felt self-conscious.

"Hello Father," I said bowing my head slightly. I knew I had to continue to act the faithful servant.

"I am so pleased you're all alright. You gave us quite a scare." It was Uncle Joe.

Who was letting all these people into my room? I pulled Eden closer to me. I think Hutch could sense my discomfort.

"I think maybe we should let Anne spend some time with Eden."

"Yes, yes, of course. We will leave your family be. Anne, you're probably hungry. I will have some food brought to you. Hutch, take care of your girls. We will check in on you again tomorrow." Jessup ushered everyone out of my room.

"How long have I been asleep?"

"About twelve hours."

"Twelve hours? Who has had Eden all this time?"

"I have. She basically slept the entire time too. You two had quite an ordeal. Didn't you?" He directed his question to the baby in a funny little voice. It made me chuckle.

"I love you," I said.

"I love you, too. I was afraid I was going to lose you both at one point. Sarah recognized right away that something was wrong and had me go to Jessup for help. There is a train they call The Sub Way that still runs on those tracks."

"Really?"

"It's only used in very special cases of emergency. Jessup ran it and they whisked us away to here."

"To where? Where is this place?"

"I'm not really sure. We didn't take The Sub Way toward The Mercatus. We went in the other direction. Not for very long but it went so fast and I was concentrating on you, so I didn't see much looking out the windows. It's very much like the monorail we use in The Estates."

I couldn't imagine it, a train underground. Eden started to fuss. She opened her eyes looking at me. It was as if she looked directly into my soul. I stared back at her. Everything about her fascinated me. She was so tiny.

"They brought you here and a woman dressed like a Coat from The Combine took care of you. Dr. Olivia Dexter was her name. They wouldn't let me stay with you so, I didn't see what happened. I was worried sick. You were in here for hours and nobody would tell me anything."

"What did you do?"

"There was nothing I could do. I paced back and forth

waiting. Uncle Joe, Jessup, and Mary Elizabeth were with me. They tried to calm me down. Finally, I couldn't take it anymore. I was about to barge in when I heard Eden's cry. It stopped me in my tracks. I waited a moment and Sarah came out to tell me you were both going to be fine." He cried holding us tight as he told me.

Eden continued to stare at me. I couldn't tell if she could actually see me. My mom told me once when Maggie was a baby and used to laugh, smile and coo when nothing was there, she was seeing her guardian angel. I thought it was weird then. Now, I thought it was sweet. Maybe that was who Eden was looking at now.

"Hello, Eden, I am your mommy. It is so nice to finally have you here with me."

She seemed to recognize my voice. Her whole body tightened up and she looked straight at me.

Hutch smiled at us stroking my hair with one arm around me resting his other hand gently on Eden. We were all on my bed together. I rested my head on him. Eden reached a tiny hand out of her tight swaddle and wrapped it around Hutch's finger. We were a family. I couldn't describe what I felt. It was more than love. More than sheer happiness. I was complete.

## Chapter 20

"Anne, Hutch?" It was Sarah knocking but not waiting to walk into my room, "Hutch, Anne, needs to get some rest. Let's let her rest."

Sarah made a move to take Eden from me.

"I feel fine." I pulled Eden closer to me. "I feel like I've been sleeping for days."

"You have a lot of medicine staving the pain away. Once those wear off, you'll be glad you got the rest when you could."

I looked at Hutch. He didn't want to leave either. Sarah again tried to take Eden away.

"No, I don't want you to take my baby. I'm fine. I don't want to be left alone. I want my family with me." I felt my eyes flare. There was no way anyone was taking my baby from me at that moment. I just got her.

"Anne, nobody is trying to take your baby from you. You just went through a lot to have Eden. Your body needs rest. You need to heal."

"Maybe you can come back in a little while?" Hutch attempted to escort Sarah out of the room.

Sarah reluctantly conceded and left.

"Anne, she's right, you do need to rest."

I'm glad he didn't say that in front of her.

"I just got her, Hutch. I'm not ready to let her go yet."

I was feeling tired, but I wasn't ready to let her go yet. Then she started to cry. How could something so small make so much noise? I started to regret not letting Sarah take her when she wanted to.

Hutch took Eden from me and started to rock her. Dancing around the room speaking soothing words to her. She stopped crying. It was sweet. My eyes were growing heavy. I didn't want to close them, I wanted to keep watching them.

"You're so good with her."

"Yeah, it feels really natural to me."

"It looks it. I hope that happens to me too."

"It will. You're going to be a great mom. Isn't she Eden?" He spoke to Eden in that same cutesy voice he used earlier. I fell in love with him all over again.

I yawned. Hutch noticed. He brought Eden over to me, "Let's let mommy get some rest, okay, Eden? Okay, daddy!" He gave Eden a little baby voice. I laughed and yawned again.

I snuggled down into the covers of the bed. Hutch kissed my forehead and offered Eden's nose for me to nuzzle. They left, shutting off the main light on their way out. I fell asleep almost immediately.

## Chapter 21

The next few days spent in the Sub Terra hospital were filled with visits from Sarah, Mary Elizabeth, Jacob, Uncle Joe, and Jessup. Along with daily exams from Dr. Olivia Dexter. She looked unusually like Dr. Kelly. Red hair pulled back in a bun, pale skin, dark-framed glasses just like her. If I didn't know any better, I would say they were sisters. She was very nice, soft-spoken, very interested in how I was feeling.

The fact was, I was feeling fine. I could see where they had made the incision to surgically remove Eden. It was a fairly long track mark across the lower part of my stomach about five or six inches. It was covered with a white piece of opaque tape. I could see a dark line and could feel staples going across closing the incision. There was very little pain compared to what I felt when I went into labor. I felt twinges when I made any movement. Dr. Dexter kept telling me to ambulate. I didn't know what she meant. Thankfully, Hutch knew what she was talking about. She wanted me to walk around. I did. A lot. She said it was extraordinary how fast I was healing and said it would be fine to return to my Dwelling.

Eden was thriving as well. She was healthy with a good loud cry which Dr. Dexter said was a sign that her lungs were strong. She was eating well too. With a clean bill of health for both of us, Hutch was able to bring us back to the Dwelling.

We took the Sub Way back. Carrying Eden swaddled in the pink blanket we got from the hospital and her tiny knitted hat protecting her head. They had fitted me with a baby sling. Eden snuggled comfortably across my chest. Mary Elizabeth, Jacob, Uncle Joe, and Jessup were all there to escort us home. They cooed over Eden. Speaking in small baby voices to her. It was weird. I couldn't wait to get back to our Dwelling and get Eden settled in her room and get away from all the attention.

We were much further away than I thought. Hutch said so as well. He didn't realize we had traveled so far. The Sub Way train was similar to The Estate monorail, but it had rows of seats. It took us back in a swoosh. I got the same feeling I did when I took the monorail for the first time in the bubble.  It seemed like a lifetime ago.

Despite our protests and claims that we would be fine, our escorts helped us get Eden inside. We walked in to see a sign hanging in our living room. "Welcome to the World Baby Eden" beneath it was a small pile of gifts.

"Just a few things to help with your first few days

here with Eden." Mary Elizabeth stood behind me with her hand on my shoulders.

"Thank you, all," I said trying to sound as gracious as possible. I just wanted to be left alone with Hutch and the baby.

"Should I open them now?"

"No, no, take your time. Introduce Eden to her room and crib. We will leave you all alone now. We will see the three of you at mass in the morning." It was Jessup. Of course, he would expect us at mass the next morning.

"Yes, we will have to start planning Eden's baptism." Jacob chimed in. I didn't know what he was talking about. I smiled and feigned a yawn.

"We should let them get settled. We will see you later." I was thankful Uncle Joe got the hint.

"Yes, thank you. Thank you all again for your kindness and generosity."

They finally left and I looked at Hutch whispering, "I didn't think they would ever leave."

Hutch closed the shutters and we went into the baby's room.

"Eden, this is your room. This is your crib. We hope you will be comfortable here."

I placed her down inside her crib. She looked up at me with a confused look on her face. It was amazing to me how expressive she was already. Her little brow furrowed, and I thought she might start crying. She didn't and I stepped back to join Hutch who was watching from the doorway.

"I think she likes it." He said putting an arm around me.

"I think I'm going to lie down for a bit. I'm suddenly very tired." It was still very early but I could barely keep my eyes open.

Hutch nodded and walked me to the bedroom, "I love you."

"I love you too. Are you happy?" I asked.

"Very." He answered.

"Me too."

## Chapter 22

Weeks passed. Despite everything, Eden's baptism was beautiful. I had never seen anything like it. I was happy we agreed to do it. Jessup told me the importance of baptizing a baby.

"It is an act of obedience symbolizing the believer's faith in a crucified, buried, and risen Savior, the believer's death to sin, the burial of the old life, and the resurrection to walk in newness of life in Christ Jesus. It is a testimony to the believer's faith in the final resurrection of the dead."

It sounded very serious. Hutch convinced me to go along with it. So, I did, and it was lovely.

We had fallen into a routine with her. Hutch did most of the late-night feedings and I took care of her during the day.

198

We were celebrating because Eden had just started sleeping through the night. I thought we were finally going to get a good night's sleep when I felt a hand over my mouth. I turned panicked to find Hutch. He wasn't in our bed next to me. I grabbed the hand over my mouth and sent my assailant sailing across the room. I was quickly out of the bed on my feet. I felt ridiculous in my nightgown trying to fight.

"Who are you? What do you want?" I demanded.

No response. It was dark, I couldn't see his face. I could make out a form. Definitely male. I lunged toward him. He retreated out of the bedroom.

I gave chase and running out into the living room. Hutch was there, gagged and tied, struggling to free himself from two men flanking him. His eyes found mine. What was happening? Looking to my right I saw another man approach me. He tried to grab me. I spun away getting in a fight stance. I had never seen these men before.

He tried to grab me again and leapt on him taking him to the ground. I rolled him over face down pulling his arm tight behind him. He cried out in pain. I shoved my knee into his back. Taking him by the hair and smashing his face down onto the concrete floor. I could hear his nose break. I kept expecting the other two men to try and help him. But I think they were too surprised. I got up to face them. The other man limp and unconscious on the ground. The look of shock and horror on the other two men's faces was almost comical. I stood at the ready anticipating their attack.

They didn't let go of Hutch who was still struggling to break free.

"Let him go, what do you want from us?"

They released Hutch who fell to his knees. The two

men got in their own odd ready stances. I quickly dispatched both of them. Now, all three men laying in a pile bloodied on our floor.

I ungagged Hutch, "the baby, they took the baby."

I ran to Eden's room. She was gone.

"Who? Who took her?" I could feel my eyes flare the way they had when Sarah tried to take Eden from me in the hospital. I untied him.

"I don't know who they were. I heard someone come into the house. I went to see what was happening and they jumped me." He pointed at two of the men lying on the floor.

"Who took her?" I wasn't panicked, I was enraged.

I used the rope that had bound Hutch's hands and feet and tied one of the unconscious men to a dining chair. I went to the kitchen and grabbed a bowl of water. I splashed him in the face to wake him up.

He woke up spitting water out of his mouth, shaking his head a confused look on his face. Grabbed a knife from the kitchen and placed it to his throat.

"Where is my baby?"

The confused look turned into terror. He started to cry.

"Tell me!" I screamed pushing the knife closer to him.

"Jessup, Jessup sent us to take the baby."

"Where?"

"The church."

"Why?"

He didn't answer. I punctured the skin of his throat with the knife. He cried out.

"I don't know. He said she is our messiah."

"What?"

"He's not going to hurt her, Anne," Hutch spoke.

"How do you know?"

"If he thinks she is their Messiah, he thinks she is very important."

"What?" I shook my head, none of it made sense to me.

"He's right, Jessup will not hurt her. Please don't kill me."

The other two men started to wake up. Using a pan from the kitchen I knocked them out again.

"What were you supposed to do with us?" Hutch was standing in front of him now.

"We were supposed to bring you to Jessup too. For the ceremony."

"What ceremony?" I was growing impatient.

"The Offering."

"What's that?" Hutch was at my side.

"It's how you will repay the flock for the kindness and generosity we've shown you." Jessup walked through the door wearing the same ceremonial garb we wore for the Exordium. He had the same crown atop his head and cross around his neck. The light from the tunnel behind him cast a glow around him. His arms spread as if he himself hung from a crucifix. "Come with me, my children. Become the Offering, the sacrificed."

"We're not going anywhere with you. Where is Eden?" I turned my knife to Jessup.

The look on his face twisted into fury, "How dare you threaten me with a weapon!"

Was this real? They were taking us to be sacrificed.

"Everyone, please calm down." Hutch stepped between us, "Father, what is happening? What are you talking about? What have you done with our daughter?"

"Sacrificium hominum, human sacrifice. It is how Sub Terra survives. It is how it has always prospered. A sacrifice to the Lord who gives us our lives and souls. Since the beginning of Sub Terra every year at harvest we must perform The Offering to ensure our existence is safe. This year is incredibly special. What you have brought us is no less than a miracle."

"You're insane, you're all insane," I screamed trying to get passed Hutch.

"Wait, Anne. Special why? Because of Eden?"

"Yes, Hutch, that is exactly why. Eden is the Second Coming. This child was conceived immaculately as Jesus was. She has come to us here in Sub Terra, not by mistake, not by accident. She was meant to be brought into this world here among us, the believers. She wasn't born out in Super Terram, not in The Dome City. She was brought into this world here in Sub Terra to bring us salvation."

The more he spoke the more enraged I became. Hutch was struggling to hold me back.

"You crazy bastard, I'll kill you." I broke free from Hutch and flew at Jessup. Before he knew what hit him, I had him on the floor with my knife at his throat. He was on his back with his hands up in surrender.

"Anne! Stop! We have to find Eden."

"Where is she?" I shouted sitting on his chest. I

pushed the knife closer to his neck.

"She's safe, we would never harm our Savior. And you could never harm me, Anne, for this is only my earthly vessel. My soul will live on without it."

"Oh yeah? Okay." I raised the knife above my head. Jessup seemed to relax underneath me, resolved to his fate. With all my anger and might I brought the knife down aiming for his chest.

Hutch stopped me, grabbing my hands above me.

"Anne, stop. You don't want his blood on your hands, believe me."

I dropped the knife. It hit the concrete with a clank.

I got off Jessup. He didn't make a move. The man tied to the chair looked on in horror. The other two men were starting to wake up.

Without a word to each other, Hutch and I ran into the bedroom to grab the bags we kept packed for our eventual escape from Sub Terra. We had packed them before Eden was born. It was always our intention to leave. We just didn't know when. Now was definitely the time. We needed to find Eden and get above ground as quickly as possible.

We opened the door running out towards the church. We were faced with an extremely agitated mob of Sub Terrans coming towards us.

"Get them!" Someone screamed. I recognized the voice as Mary Elizabeth's.

I looked at Hutch. They blocked our only way to Eden. Hutch looked hopeless. Jessup came out of our Dwelling followed by the three men sent to kidnap us. There was only one direction to go. We turned and ran away from them following the tracks on our right. We ran as fast as we could, our bare feet slapping against the concrete. I felt ridiculous in my nightgown. We didn't know where we were going.

We took the first tunnel we saw to our left. A long strip of fluorescent lights flickered as we ran. The walls made of concrete bricks were covered with graffiti. It was quiet. The only sound our heavy breathing and the hum of the lights above us. We had outrun them for the time being.

We made our way down the eerie hallway hoping to find another way around to the church.

"Do you see that?" I whispered.

"What?"

"Someone is coming, there, ahead of us." I pointed down the tunnel.

There was nowhere to go. Whoever it was, they were coming fast. I got in a ready stance cursing my inappropriate clothing.

Hutch stood next to me looking scared. The person got closer. I started to hear our other pursuers as well. My heart was pounding. I could swear I heard Hutch's too. At least our new enemy was alone. Tired of waiting for him to reach us. I went on the attack. I stopped in my tracks as soon as I saw him.

## Chapter 23

"Uncle Joe?" I couldn't believe my eyes. It was Uncle Joe and he had Eden in his arms.

"We have to go!" He handed me Eden.

She was in the sling I brought her home from the hospital in. I strapped her to me. "Where are we going?"

"Just trust me!"

Hutch and I followed Uncle Joe down the long tunnel to another narrower tunnel. We traveled down into the depths of Sub Terra. I couldn't imagine where he was taking us. Eden strapped safely to my chest. The motion of us running lulled her to sleep. I held Hutch's hand; Uncle Joe held my other hand. I didn't trust him like I used to, but I didn't have a choice now. It was stay and be sacrificed to the crazed mob chasing us or go with him to a place unknown.

We went down flights of stairs. It was getting darker and darker as we went. We finally reached the very bottom, with nowhere left to go.

"Get in, get in!" He shouted.

We got into a small vehicle pod. It closed around us. It was cramp, not made for the cargo it currently held.

Uncle Joe pulled a lever and the floor opened beneath us sending us falling for what felt like an eternity. My stomach was in my throat, I held Eden tight.

With a loud splash, we hit water hard. Anticipating the pod to fill with water I grabbed tighter hold of Eden. Uncle Joe pulled another lever and we were engulfed, water surrounding us. Hutch looked at me with fear in his eyes. We plunged deeper into the water.

"What are you doing?" I asked bracing myself for whatever was coming next.

"I'm taking you to Atlantica."

# Epilogue

## *ATLANTICA*

"Sir, I believe everything is proceeding as it should be."

A young soldier dressed in a gray uniform approached a man seated at the helm of the bridge.

Enormous plexiglass windows gave view to the vast ocean surrounding them in blue.  The glow of lights from the Vessels below illuminated the glass floor beneath them.

"Excellent.  Have the First Gens arrived?"

"Yes, Flannery Five reported he has them in Docking Bay Three."

"Seems fitting Flannery Five would be the one to bring them in."

"Sir?"

"Flannery Two was a founding father of Atlantica along with the first in my line Dexter One and the others."

"Others, Sir?"

"Do you know nothing of our history, young man?"

The tall slender twenty-something stared blankly at the older man.

"Atlantica was founded, designed, built and completed by seven men in 2025. When they heard whispers of The Shift, they decided to pool their resources and Atlantica was born to escape the effects of The Shift. That's the abridged version of the story. I'll have to see what they're teaching you kids at The Academy these days. You should know this."

"I'm sorry, sir."

"No apologies, if you don't know, you weren't taught, and we need everyone to study and remember our origins.  But we don't have time for that now, let's go, it's time to meet the Chosen Ones."

* * * * *

One Season Book 3: Atlantica will be available soon.

Made in United States
North Haven, CT
08 July 2023

38729159R00120